The Fox Cub Bold

Then he scolded himself for his regrets. Was this the correct attitude at the first setback for a brave young fox who had chosen an independent path – who had *yearned* for complete freedom? Of course not. But then, this was more than a setback. He hadn't reckoned on becoming crippled in his fine new life. But perhaps he wasn't crippled – it was too early to be sure of that. And anyway, he should count himself lucky to be still alive. But . . . but . . . what was the good of being alive if one was crippled? For a young fox that would be a living death. Yet . . . this was the first true test of his character. He *mustn't* fail himself. He must be resolute; determined to overcome his difficulties. . . .

The Fox Cub Bold

Colin Dann

Illustrated by Terry Riley

Beaver Books

A Beaver Book
Published by Arrow Books Limited
17-21 Conway Street, London W1P 6JD

An imprint of the Hutchinson Publishing Group

London Melbourne Sydney Auckland
Johannesburg and agencies throughout
the world

First published by Hutchinson 1983
Beaver edition 1984

Printed and bound in Great Britain by
Anchor Brendon Limited, Tiptree, Essex

ISBN 0 09 937520 6

Contents

For Cathryn, Matthew and Tara

—1—
The Real World

The summer sun shone, wide and warm, on the country-side. The fox cub Bold saw the broad horizon lit by its golden rays and narrowed his eyes against the glare. He felt he stood in the midst of a new world. The rolling downland and its scattered coverings of woodland and bracken were spread before him and around him.

'This is the real world,' he whispered to himself. 'The wide, wild natural world.' In all the expanse the only movement to be detected was the restless flight of a bird here and there or the lazy waving of greenery caused by the slightest of breezes. The cub repeated his phrase to himself in a delighted murmur – 'the real world, the real world. . . .' The spirit of adventure that had filled him as he had stepped outside the limits of the Nature Reserve where his family lived sharpened to a new pitch. He leapt forward and raced across the turf, glorying in his own health and vigour. His eyes sparkled, the blood sang in his veins – he felt as free as the air.

From a tree-top a solitary magpie was watching. 'Here's a topsy-turvy creature,' it muttered. 'A fox out parading in the daytime for all to see, and a young one too. His parents didn't teach *him* stealth. Humph!' he rasped. 'He'll learn the hard way, I suppose.'

Bold was not fooled by the temporarily empty landscape. His father had told him enough about life outside the haven of the Park for him to appreciate its dangers. And who knew more of such things than his father, the fox from Farthing Wood? For he had travelled across this country, leading his assorted band of animals and birds from the destruction of their old woodland home to a new future in the protected Reserve. On the journey all the creatures, strong and weak alike, had been bound by a sworn oath – a pledge to help and defend each other. This had continued after their arrival in the Reserve and had been maintained by them all ever since. But Bold relished his feeling of complete independence. He had confidence in the strength of his body and, as for his character, well, his parents had not chosen his name for nothing. The narrow limits of White Deer Park were not for him. He had decided to live the True Wild Life – accepting its thrills and its perils alike.

A bank vole started in his path and went scurrying away through the grass stems. Bold checked his headlong career. But it was some moments before he reminded himself that any game, big or small, was now prey to his hunting skill. He owed no loyalties, no allegiances here. No animals in the real world were bound by the oath. By the time he set off again the little beast had disappeared from sight. Bold made no attempt to hunt for it, deciding it was probably already cowering inside its bolt-hole. He went on now at a slower pace, sniffing the pungent air and carefully scanning the terrain for any sign of life.

The magpie continued to view his progress, noting the vole's escape. 'Not a great hunter, it seems,' it had said to itself. 'Well, he'll have to do better than that or *he* won't survive long.' It flew away to another tree, chack-chacking loudly as it went.

Bold looked up at the sound. The startling black and white of the bird's wings flashed like a signal against the sky's hazy blue. It landed on a branch, its long tail dipping and rising to maintain its balance. As Bold trotted on, the bird flew off again to investigate something that interested it on the ground. The cub saw it begin to peck at the object of interest, tugging with its bill this way and that in its efforts to free a morsel.

Bold recalled his own empty stomach. He had not eaten since leaving White Deer Park, and now here, perhaps, was a mouthful or two for the taking. He was more than a match for any bird. He had only to run forward. . . .

As he dashed up, the magpie rose awkwardly into the air, uttering a scolding, irritated cry. Bold discovered the mutilated remains of a long-dead wood pigeon. As he was by no means averse to a meal of carrion, whatever its rankness, he snapped at the skin and bone eagerly.

The angry magpie eyed him from a nearby vantage point, wondering if he would leave anything. In the end it could not contain its frustration. 'Is this your idea of hunting?' it screeched down at him. 'The foxes in this area prefer to rely on their skill in stalking *live* quarry. They roam at night when we birds have long since tucked our heads under our wings. Any real fox would turn up its nose at a poor scrap like that.'

Bold looked up in astonishment. The reference to a

'real fox' certainly jarred on him. 'Where I come from I was taught not to ignore any source of food that might mean the difference between eating and going hungry,' he returned. 'But I can assure you I know all about night foraging.'

'Really?' said the magpie sarcastically. 'But I suppose it's easier for you to snatch a meal from a being weaker than yourself?'

'I'm not in the habit of doing such a thing,' Bold replied, 'though I'm certain most creatures would accept it as one of the laws of nature – unfair as it seems to you.'

'Unfair and greedy,' remarked the magpie.

'Well, you've made your point,' said Bold. 'As it happens, there's really nothing but feathers left on this carcass anyway. So I'll gladly relinquish the morsel.'

The magpie, somewhat mollified, said: 'Is it your habit to be abroad in the daytime?'

'Habit? No. I'm no different from other foxes in enjoying the greater security of the dark. I've been exploring my new domain.'

'*Domain?*' echoed the magpie. 'If you see this area as your domain you're in for a few surprises, my youngster.'

'I doubt it,' said Bold confidently. 'I have as much right to roam here as any other creature. I accept their rights so they should accept mine.'

'Oh, they should, should they?' said the magpie, letting out a cynical chuckle. 'Well, we shall see. I wasn't only referring to other beats, I might tell you.'

'Of course, you mean humans,' Bold answered, quite unperturbed. 'Well, they're not exactly unfamiliar to me, either.'

The magpie shook its head. 'I don't know where you have travelled from, 'it said, 'but your over-confidence makes me think it must be somewhere a lot less fraught with danger than this quarter. If I'm right in my view, you'd do well not to stay around here too long.'

Bold laughed. 'My very motive for coming here was a quest for adventure,' he said naively. 'I want to be a part of the real world.'

The magpie was scornful. 'Then you might get more than you bargain for,' he retorted. 'You obviously know nothing of what you speak about.' And he flew away, impatient with the cub's presumption.

Bold was amused. 'Well, I must have upset him,' he murmured. 'Perhaps we'll meet again some time when he might have changed his tune. I'm a creature of *quite* a different stamp from the one he takes me for.' He ran on, dauntless as ever. He looked back once, and was quick to notice that the bird had returned to the disputed remains of the pigeon.

—2—
The Bold Young Fox

That night, after a short nap, Bold did indeed go hunting.
The air was warm and still as he entered a small wood. He
came to a spot where there was a thick covering of
ground-ivy. Amongst this vegetation the rustlings and
scurryings of small animals could clearly be heard. Bold
set himself to catch his supper.

Half in sport and half in earnest, he spent a good part
of the night tracking and pouncing on the less lucky of
those shrews and mice who were engaged on their own
urgent quests for food. His hunger finally satisfied, the
cub curled himself up under a holly bush, his head on his
paws, and fell gratefully asleep.

Although he was well concealed from human scrutiny,
Bold's presence in the wood was well noted by the wild

night creatures, large and small, as they ambled amongst the trees or flew overhead on their particular errands. To some, he represented a competitor, to others, an additional danger to heed. Certainly, by daybreak the existence of a strange young fox in the neighbourhood was common knowledge to the wood's population. Bold, of course, remained blissfully unaware of the interest he had attracted.

He awoke late in the day. He got up and stretched elaborately. A pool of water on a patch of ground dotted with sedges attracted his attention. Bold quenched his thirst, lapping the water slowly while his eyes took in his surroundings. Already his old home was forgotten. There was so much to explore, so many new sensations awaiting him. Eagerly he trotted off towards the boundaries of the wood, feeling strong and refreshed.

Another bright, sunny August day greeted him as he emerged into the open downland. On the threshold of this gloriously wide expanse he paused briefly to look about him. Again, empty countryside met his gaze. Joyfully, confidently, he went loping along. The warnings of the magpie on the previous day seemed meaningless in such a landscape.

Later a sole human figure appeared on the horizon, accompanied by a dog no bigger than Bold himself. The fox did not even change his direction. His easy, even lope brought him within fifty metres of the two. The man watched him pass. The dog, intent on a particularly rich mix of scents on the ground, ignored him completely. Bold was exhilarated. He felt invincible; equal to any challenge.

He encountered no more human figures but, as he ran through some long grass, he flushed a skylark from its vulnerable nest on the open ground. The mother bird soared high into the air, uttering its cry of alarm. Bold had not yet tasted eggs so, fortunately for the lark, he did not know that they were good to eat. He ran on with an excited yap and the speckled, white eggs were soon once more covered by the warm breast feathers of their parent.

Everywhere he ran, birds would fly up out of his path. Rabbits, browsing close to their burrows, would bolt instantly at his approach. Bold came to feel the stature of being the most powerful member of the indigenous wildlife, feared and respected by all others. Only another fox or, perhaps, a badger could rival his position of supremacy. Small wonder that his self-confidence was unbounded. Should he see that magpie again he would laugh in its face!

By dusk he had travelled a considerable distance. He looked forward to the night's hunt and hoped for more exciting prey than before to test his skills. But first he must rest. There was a tiny stream running across country at this point – just a ribbon of water over which he could easily leap. An ancient, solitary hawthorn stood on one bank, its lower boughs almost dipping themselves into the rivulet. Bold made straight for this tree and settled himself comfortably under its umbrella of foliage.

He did not sleep at once but remained watchful. The evening song of birds preparing to go to roost pierced the still air. The metallic cough of a pheasant rang out periodically. No thought of his friends, his brother and sister cubs, nor even of his redoubtable father, entered Bold's thoughts. Only the vaguest picture of Vixen, his mother, flitted across his mind's eye. He remembered the way she had taught him to stalk his quarry in the Nature Reserve as he remembered her lithe, supple motion.

He was startled from his drowsy state (though hoped he hadn't shown it) by the sound of what was obviously a large bird making its landing in the crown of the hawthorn. Bold barked warningly but, to his surprise, the bird stayed where it was. It let out an answering 'caw', safe in the knowledge that it was well out of reach, and peered through the interlocking branches.

'Oh-ho!' it cried. 'So here's the bold young fox. I've seen you off and on today.'

Bold looked up, but the darkness of the bird's body was almost totally obscured by the gathering night. He realized his companion was a Carrion Crow, as black as soot from its beak-tip to its feet.

'You flatter me by your interest,' replied Bold bluntly.

'A large creature like you could hardly be missed in the daylight,' returned the crow, 'and I must express my gratitude to you.'

'Gratitude? Whatever for?'

'Finding a meal for me. The lark's eggs you spurned soon filled *my* stomach.'

'Each to his own habits,' said Bold and yawned.

'And *your* habits seem to be unique among foxes,' remarked the crow.

Bold sighed. 'You mean my daytime activity?' he asked patiently.

'Exactly.'

'What's so unusual about it?' protested the fox cub. 'It's not unknown for foxes to be about in the daylight.'

'Round here it is,' said the crow succinctly.

'Well, it isn't where *I* come from,' Bold persisted, 'and I can see no reason why I shouldn't continue to explore my surroundings whenever I feel like it. You birds are a nervous lot – always on the move, never still for more than a moment. You seem to read danger into everything.'

The crow ignored Bold's last remarks. 'Where *do* you come from?' it inquired.

Bold hesitated. If he mentioned the Nature Reserve, he

would only be inviting a sarcastic comment from the bird. 'Oh – er – a good distance away,' he said vaguely.

'Things may be different there,' said the crow. 'There *are* places, I believe, where human beings are not allowed to intrude on the freedom of wild creatures. But I've never been in any.'

Bold did not know if the crow was making a clever guess at his origins. In any case he disregarded it. 'Well, I've seen nothing to fear in these parts in the way of human presence,' he boasted.

'Then you've been very fortunate,' the crow observed. 'But I warn you – there are some days when the whole countryside is full of them.'

'I'm grateful for your warning,' said Bold. 'But I'm quite able to look after myself. And now, if you have no objection, I'll compose myself to sleep.'

'Don't mind me,' said the crow. 'I'm about to settle down as well.'

The next few days seemed to support Bold's assertion that there was nothing to fear. As before, human appearances on the downland were restricted to infrequent sightings by the cub. Single figures, a couple or, at the most, three together. He kept well clear of those and on these times did not range so far. He had found a good hunting territory to which he returned again and again. The fine weather continued.

Then one day, while the cub was actually lying among some bracken sunning himself, his safe empty world suddenly took on a new character. He was at the top of a small rise of ground, and up this rise, coming straight towards him, was a large party of people, about thirty in number. They were a party of ramblers and they advanced quickly. Bold had no time to hide himself, and anyway the ferns thereabouts were neither thick enough nor tall enough to have served as a screen. For the first time the young fox knew himself to be frightened. He had never before in his life seen such a large number of people together.

As he jumped up to run, the first among the group spotted him and immediately pointed him out to all the rest, with enthusiastic cries and gestures. Of course they meant him no harm. He was merely an object of interest. The sound of their raised voices alarmed Bold even more and he dashed blindly hither and thither in panic, getting amongst their feet and almost succeeding in tripping some of them up. At last he saw a clear space ahead and raced towards it, expecting every moment that the terrifying mass of people would give chase. In his ignorance of humans he had absolutely no idea that he could easily outrun any of them.

He turned his head fearfully as he ran and was amazed to see his discoverers standing stock still, calmly watching his escape. The next time he turned they had gone on their way. Bold stopped running.

When he had recovered from the danger of his first encounter with man, he took stock of his situation. It seemed to him that, once again, the threat of danger had turned out to be groundless. His relief was tremendous. His self-confidence took another boost but this, for Bold, was to prove to be his real danger.

— 3 —

The Game Wood

Over the next few weeks Bold ranged wide and far. He entered an area of human habitation – of farmland and scattered hamlets. He had attained his full size and was a splendid specimen of a male fox. He was well-built, muscular, with a beautifully healthy coat and brush; he was also clean-limbed and able to run quite tirelessly at a considerable speed. Though he had the sense not to stray too close to the man-made buildings and dwellings, he had developed a fearlessness of his only real enemy which amounted to arrogance. His innate cunning and cleverness were more than a match for Man's.

Food was plentiful and his diet was a varied one. On one occasion he killed a cock partridge as it rose from the ground in front of him. From that moment on he acquired a taste for game. In his nightly hunting forays his continual searchings took him to every corner of the district, but he was not often successful. Then one evening he came to a place where the scent of game seemed to hang in the air. It was a wooded area entirely fenced off from the surrounding countryside, but the fence was old, warped and damaged and no obstacle to a determined young fox.

Inside the boundary there was evidence of the scent of Man. Where the ground was soft and damp the unmistakable marks of his trail were plain to see, but Bold had no concern for it. He was on the track of something of far more interest. His mouth watered freely in anticipation of the delicious meal that awaited him. Cautiously, noiselessly, he stole through the undergrowth. He knew his quarry was not far away.

Under a thick cover of bramble a hen pheasant was disturbed from her rest. Bold pounced and, with a quick snap of his powerful young jaws, all was over. That night he feasted handsomely.

There was a large beech tree standing on a hump of ground, the roots of which were partially exposed. Underneath the roots an invitingly secluded hole attracted Bold's notice. He sniffed carefully all around and inside it. The smell of badger was very strong, but no sound could be heard and Bold decided the occupants were away from home. He had no fear of badger. An old male animal – a close companion of his father's – had figured largely in his early life in the Reserve. Bold went inside the hole and along the tunnel for a few paces before curling up to sleep.

Towards morning he awoke instantly at the approach of the owner of the set. Bold prepared to leave his makeshift den – it had served his purpose well. At the entrance to the tunnel a sow badger was standing uncertainly, sniffing the air around her home with caution. An encounter with a fox was not one to be undertaken without hesitation.

But Bold was disposed to be friendly. 'Please don't be alarmed,' he said. 'I certainly mean no harm.'

'Are you alone?' the badger asked nervously.

'Quite alone,' Bold replied.

'Foxes and badgers tend to keep apart in this wood,' she went on. 'That must be why I've never seen you before.'

'No. I'm a stranger hereabouts,' Bold told her. 'I only found the spot by chance.'

'Then I can guess your reason for coming here.'

'I was led here by my nose.' Bold explained jocularly.

'Yes, a lot of foxes come for the same reason,' remarked the badger. 'Most of them don't stay long, however.'

'Competition?' asked the cub.

'You could say that,' she answered, 'though it's not the sort of competition you're thinking of.'

'What then?'

'Haven't you seen the footprints?'

'Oh, yes. But I paid no attention to them,' he bragged.

'You'd be foolish not to,' she said. 'They're your real competition.'

'Humans?'

'Of course. Why do you think the wood is so rich in game birds?'

'It didn't occur to me.'

'Well, I'll tell you,' said the badger. 'They're released here by men for *their* use.'

'Use? I don't understand,' said Bold. 'Do *they* eat them?'

'I believe so. At any rate, they hunt them.'

'Hm.' Bold pondered. 'No wonder foxes don't often choose to stay. But you – you've made your home here!'

'*I'm* comparatively safe,' she said. 'I'm not so inclined to drool over pheasant and they – the humans I mean – seem to know that.'

'I see. But there don't seem to be any men about at present, so perhaps I'll risk staying on.'

'They haven't started hunting yet. But, let me warn you, you *would* be running a risk. There is one human who is always around here keeping an eye open for anything that might be after his precious birds.'

'Oh – one! I'm sure I'm capable of dealing with him,' Bold said easily.

'Yes, well – maybe. But summer's on the wane and *that's* a sign that they'll soon be coming in force. They flush the birds out of these coverts and shoot them in the open. And when *that* happens, woe betide any other creature who may be around. We're *all* game then.'

'I'll worry about that when it happens,' Bold said lightly. 'Thank you for your advice – and your warm den.'

The badger brushed past him. 'Very well,' she said. 'But just remember – it *is* my set.'

'As you say,' he acknowledged, and went on his way.

Bold paid some heed to the she-badger's warning by leaving the enclosure during the daylight hours to continue his explorations. But when night fell again, he returned. Ears cocked for the faintest sound of human tread, the cub set out to track down his second victim.

Now that the scent of fox – a new fox – had spread through the wood, the nervous game birds were not so easily caught napping. But there was one creature who had been injured previously by a stoat and was unable to fly. Bold made short work of him. And, in the succeeding nights, Bold's desire to test his hunting skills was more than satisfied.

As time went on he became expert in the pursuit of pheasant and, although he was not always successful in catching his favourite prey, his appetite was only increased by failure. So a pattern was established in his life which, for a week or two, did not change.

Each evening he left the wider area of farmland and entered the enclosed wood. He never came face to face with the gamekeeper, but both were very much aware of the other's existence. When danger threatened, Bold always managed to elude his enemy.

From time to time the young fox came across the sow badger or one of her family. They showed surprise that he continued to thrive in their wood but he swept their astonishment aside contemptuously. He became prouder than ever of his skill and began to believe he really did have exceptional abilities.

One night, when his usual luck deserted him, Bold decided to investigate a fresh corner of the wood. In this quarter, in addition to the mouth-watering smell of pheasant, Bold detected a new, ranker odour. He soon discovered it source. Hanging from a line attached to the enclosing fence an assortment of rotting carcasses swayed slightly in the night air. The grisly collection was comprised mostly of birds such as crows and rooks, but the decomposing bodies of a weasel and a stoat were also included. Bold realized at once he was looking at the handiwork of his enemy the gamekeeper.

He stood, horrified but fascinated by the sight. To his keen nose, the smell was overpowering. The bodies had obviously been hanging there a long time to warn off would-be attackers of the precious game birds. No fox, or the remains of a fox, was among the grotesque collection. Bold was exultant. The man held no sway over his kind. These were small fry – weaker creatures unable to look out for themselves. But a fox such as he was a different matter. No human was capable of meddling in his affairs.

Shortly afterwards he caught his prey. He did not carry it under cover to devour in safety. He took it to the gamekeeper's 'gibbet' and slowly, brazenly, he consumed it, underneath those quivering trophies. Only a handful of feathers and bones were left behind as evidence of his defiance.

—4—
The True Wild Life

The next night Bold entered the wood with extreme caution. For, unimpressed by the gibbet, he was still realistic enough to expect the gamekeeper to react in some way to his gesture of contempt. As he crept along, not far from the badgers' home, a sharp cry of pain rent the air, followed by grunts and snorts of a most distressing kind. Bold hastened towards the sound and, along one of his regular paths, he found the sow badger caught fast in a horrible metal trap. The more she struggled, the more its vice-like grip seemed to increase. A strong, noose-like wire bore down upon her back, making her gasp for breath and almost threatening to cripple her.

Bold sniffed gingerly at the snare, preparing to leap

away on the instant if it threatened him too. The poor she-badger, panting painfully, looked at him with dull, hopeless eyes. The cub was convinced this trap had been sprung for him, and that the luckless badger had blundered into it instead. Quite unknowingly, she had saved him from almost certain death. He stood heavily in her debt. He looked more closely at the man-made device.

'I'm going to try to help you,' he told the badger coolly. 'Keep quite still.'

The trapped animal had already ceased to struggle. The pain was too severe. She heard Bold's words in amazement. What could he mean? Why didn't he run away while he was still safe? The strongest of all instincts for any wild creature on its own was self-preservation. *She* had been caught, not he. She continued to cower where she was, unable to answer him.

Bold had discovered that the strong wire that was pinning her body so cruelly to the ground was the only obstacle to her freedom. Once inside, it was impossible for the ensnared beast to free itself, for the wire could not be reached over its own back. But, from outside the trap, the wire could be sprung or snapped. Bold's only tool was the strength of his jaws.

'I'll bite this wire,' he muttered to the badger, but half to himself. He tried to get a grip on it, but it pressed too deep into her flesh and it was impossible for him to get his teeth round it without wounding her. A harsh gasp of pain escaped her lips at his first attempt. He tried again at another point. Again she winced in agony, closing her eyes. Frustrated, Bold withdrew temporarily.

He sniffed the air, while his ears constantly strained for a sound of the trap-setter. All seemed quiet. He moved forward again with increased determination. Now he noticed that at one end of the wire there was a short piece that did not pass over the sow badger's back. He fastened his side teeth on it and bit hard. Absolutely nothing happened.

'This may take a long time,' he said. 'But we have the entire night ahead of us.'

The sow badger lay fatalistically at the gamekeeper's mercy. She listened, in a quite uncomprehending manner, to the rasping of Bold's fangs on the wire. What was he doing it for, when in all probability the result would only be injury to himself as well? The night hours slowly crept by.

As Bold made one of his several pauses to rest his aching jaws, he thought he heard a steady tramp . . . tramp in the distance. He froze, his every nerve and muscle quivering with tension. Yes, there was no doubt of it. Something was approaching, and that regular tread could only be the sound of human footsteps. The gamekeeper was coming to assess his handiwork!

Bold attacked the wire with renewed ferocity and desperation, knowing that at any moment he would have to flee. Then, quite suddenly, the weakened wire snapped with a fierce backward lash that nearly blinded him. Almost at the same moment, the badger pulled herself clear and, instinctively, ran straight for her set. Bold raced after her.

In the deeper darkness of the lair they lay panting side by side. Bold's eye streamed with water and, in one corner, a thin trickle of blood ran where the point of the severed wire had pierced. The badger's back, too, had been cut and throbbed insistently.

'Why? Why?' she kept muttering.

Bold did not answer, but rubbed his bad eye with the back of one paw as if it would heal it.

Overcome by their experiences, they fell into an uneasy sleep.

The sow badger awoke first. Her back still smarted, but the realization that she was still alive flooded over her joyously. It was as though she had cheated death. But – no! *She* hadn't cheated it. She remembered her companion. She smelt the blood on his face and began to lick at his fur, gently and with gratitude. Bold awoke and shook his head in an attempt to free himself of the pain.

'*Why* did you do it?' she asked him.

He looked at her for a moment. 'That trap was laid for me,' he replied.

The badger still couldn't fathom his meaning. 'Surely, then,' she faltered, 'that was your escape?'

'Yes,' he said. 'I escaped death – because of you.'

'Then why should I live?' she persisted in bewilderment.

Now it was Bold's turn to have no understanding. 'But why should you *die*,' he emphasized, 'because of my good fortune?'

'That's Life,' she answered in a matter-of-fact way.

'No. That's Death,' he corrected her. 'And too great a sacrifice.'

'My carelessness led me into the trap,' said the badger. 'I had only myself to blame.'

'I owed it to you to help *you* to escape as long as I ran free,' Bold tried to explain. But he could see that she still didn't understand. Was this, then, the True Wild Life after all? This natural indifference to another's suffering, even to another's fate, when the cause of it had been oneself? In *his* upbringing, the law instilled by his father and enshrined in the oath, had been to help one's friends in trouble, and to expect the same from them. But even there, in the Nature Reserve, he seemed to remember that the law only applied to a particular group of creatures – those animals and birds who had banded together long ago to travel across country to the safety of the Park.

The badger interrupted his thoughts. 'I shall be forever grateful to you,' she was saying, 'and I'm now very much in *your* debt.' She paused. 'If I follow your example – and it seems I must – I offer you my help, and that of my clan, if ever you need it.'

'I am glad I freed you,' said Bold simply. 'And I –

'And you've wounded yourself in doing so, I fear to say,' she broke in.

'It will heal,' he said.

'Does my licking help?' she asked him.

'It does soothe,' he answered.

She resumed her task.

'Tomorrow I move on,' the cub said decisively. 'This episode has taught me I shouldn't linger here.'

'You are wise,' she answered.

'But first,' said Bold with bravado, 'I shall have one more meal of pheasant.'

'And I,' responded the badger, 'shall help you catch it.'

—5—

Humans Can Be Dangerous

Bold's last taste of game in the wood passed off without further interruption by the keeper. He and the sow badger made their farewells and the cub parted from her, urging her to be more cautious than before.

His eye still pained him and it tended to water, so that his vision was a little impaired. But, in spite of the injury, he had escaped the clutches of Man – indeed had bested him – and continued to lead what seemed to him to be a charmed life. However, Bold was to discover that he had tarried a little too long in the area.

He found a thicket of gorse which was ideal to lie up in during the day. It was within the farmland, but in open

country, and it became his regular refuge. He marked it
carefully in several places to proclaim his ownership.
One morning, soon afterwards, he woke to the sound
of gunfire.

He jumped up and, keeping under cover, looked out
across the terrain. A line of men, all with firearms, stood
at intervals of some metres along the crest of a slight
ridge. Birds were wheeling in the sky, flying in panic from
the death that stalked them below. Reports of gunfire
were repeated regularly and a good number of the birds
suddenly crumpled up in flight and crashed headlong to
the ground. Fresh stocks of partridge, beaten from the
open country, and pheasants, roused from the nearby
copses where they had been released when young, came
flying overhead in wave after wave. The men, raising their
weapons, dealt destruction on all sides. The shooting
season was in full swing.

Bold remembered the sow badger's remarks about no
living thing being safe when guns were around. The
awful crack! crack! of the hideous machines terrified the
young fox. Should he run or stay under cover? Suddenly
a pheasant plummeted to earth with a muffled thump
right under his nose and then he saw a large dog coming
for it. His mind was made up.

Avoiding the path of the retriever, he dashed away
from the gorse patch at full stretch and away, as he
thought, from the gunfire. As he ran his bad eye watered
abominably and it was this that caused him to make a
fatal mistake. He seemed to be running in a mist and he
was almost on the second line of guns before he saw
them. One of the sportsmen, who was in the act of
reloading, gave a shout to his companions as Bold came
up. A fox was fair game when their minds were on
slaughter and, as Bold veered sharply in mortal fear, he
saw one man raise his weapon and take aim at him. The

fox increased his speed, heard a sharp crack! behind and, the next instant, felt a fierce sear of pain in his right thigh. Bold fell.

The sportsman cried out triumphantly. Before anything more could happen, a new covey of partridges came overhead and, mercifully, engaged the men's attention. Bold pulled himself up. He could put no weight on his wounded leg which felt quite numb until he tried to stand. Then a fresh surge of pain shot through him. Instinctively, he resorted to his three good legs and so, half dragging the injured one along the ground because he couldn't lift it, he limped slowly and wonkily across the field. Every moment he expected the impact of the second gunshot which would finish him off. But it didn't come. Luckily for him, the game in the air was better sport.

It seemed an age – an eternity – before he had dragged himself to a sort of safety, collapsing into a drainage ditch. His leg bled freely and was throbbing unmercifully. A trickle of water in the ditch bottom cooled him a little and he drank some of it. Though he didn't know it, the lead shot from the gun had passed right through his thigh which was very fortunate but, in doing so, had ripped the muscle drastically. He dared not stay still for long and so he began to limp along the ditch where at least he was out of sight.

The ditch ran right through one of the spinneys, but Bold pulled himself out of it when he reached the comparative obscurity of the overhanging trees. Now he had to find proper cover – and quickly. He made straight for a thick clump of bramble, hauling himself through the tearing briars to its very heart. He felt weak and dizzy and had scarcely enough strength left to lick the blood from his fur.

The noise of gunfire, though quieter in here, continued

unabated. Bold's greatest fear now was of the dogs. Would they come tracking him? He guessed that a trail of blood led right up to his hideout. No dog could fail to unearth him if once put on his scent. There was nothing he could do but wait. He had no means of defending himself. If the dogs came it would be the end of him, he knew, and the best that could be hoped for then would be a quick death. Bold tried to remain alert but his weak state induced an uncontrollable drowsiness and he drifted into unconsciousness.

When he awoke it was dark. He had no idea how long he had slept but all was peaceful again. No guns, no dogs. The blood around his wound had dried and his fur was caked with it. He tried to raise himself, eager to test the leg, but it had stiffened so much that he could not even bend it. He sank back again, wondering what on earth to do. He was not hungry but his feverishness had caused a raging thirst. He lay a little longer, feeling unutterably dejected and lonely. It was at such a time, he reflected, that one hankered for companionship – of any sort. Now he wished that his brother cub, Friendly, were with him. *He* would have tried to lift his spirits.

Then he scolded himself for his regrets. Was this the correct attitude at the first setback for a brave young fox who had chosen an independent path – who had *yearned* for complete freedom? Of course not. But then, this was more than a setback. He hadn't reckoned on becoming crippled in his fine new life. But perhaps he wasn't crippled – it was too early to be sure of that. And anyway, he should count himself lucky to be still alive. But . . . but . . . what was the good of being alive if one was crippled? For a young fox that would be a living death. Yet . . . this was the first true test of his character. He *mustn't* fail himself. He must be resolute; determined to overcome his difficulties . . . . His thoughts ran round and round in his mind until he dozed again.

The next time his eyes opened, it was still dark. Bold's thirst was now so pressing that he knew that somehow he must move himself from that place to find water. He dragged himself from the midst of the bramble bush, trailing his bad leg. Once in the open part of the wood, he tried again to stand on all four paws. Again the wounded leg collapsed under him. The pain was too great to bear. Bold gritted his teeth and hobbled forward on three legs. He found a puddle in a dip in the ground and lapped at it greedily. For a long time he drank until his tremendous thirst was assuaged. Then he sat down awkwardly, taking care that his weight rested on his good side.

Well, here was a fine situation! An animal who relied on speed and stealth to catch his prey and who now wouldn't be able to pounce even if he could get close enough to it! There could be no more hunting trips for a bit. Insects, worms and fruit were the best he could hope for. However, at least his eye no longer hurt him, though it did still run.

Oh, he *was* hungry. He cast around a bit, saw nothing, and then he remembered the bramble clump. He eased himself upright and limped back to his hideaway. The bush was loaded with ripe blackberries. Here, at any rate, was some sort of a meal.

Bold was busy garnering the fruit which really required very little effort when he saw a movement among the thorny stems. A dormouse was engaged on the same errand, sitting on its haunches while it delicately nibbled a berry in its front paws. Oblivious of the large animal's presence, it systematically turned the fruit round with its little claws to get at the best bits, then discarded the remains to search for a fresh one. Bold held himself still.

The creature presented a welcome addition to his meal if only he could catch it. He watched the mouse come closer and closer. At last it was within range. Bold lunged forward, snapping his jaws. They closed on thin air. The dormouse jumped in fright onto the ground in front of him, and then scuttled away. Bold limped hopelessly after it. Of course it was too fast for him and ran up the trunk of an elder shrub. Once safely out of reach it sat, quivering, on a stem and looked down at him with its black, bead-like eyes.

'You're lucky I'm injured,' the fox said grudgingly, 'otherwise you wouldn't be sitting up there, I can tell you.'

'If you can't catch a mouse, you'll soon starve to death,' replied the escaped animal.

'Don't you be too sure,' said Bold. 'I'll search you out in the daytime when you're asleep.'

'You'd never find me,' chirped the dormouse. 'I'll be way out of your reach.'

'Just you wait till my leg's mended. Then you won't be so cocky!'

'Oh yes, I'll sit around here until that happens, shall I?' the dormouse said derisively.

Bold scowled. 'You'll be my first mouthful when I'm fit again, I promise you that,' he snarled. He was furious at being on the defensive before this tiny creature.

But the dormouse continued to look steadfastly at him as if he were of no more account than a piece of dead wood. Bold turned away and had the mortification of having to display his awful limp in all its detail as he went. He had to content himself with settling down again to his meagre meal of blackberries.

A shower of rain in the early morning brought out the worms and snails and Bold was really quite glad of the chance to gobble up a number of them. The cool dampness of the day refreshed him and seemed to soothe the constant nagging pain in his right leg. But with the onset of daylight he crept back to his lair amongst the thorns to nurse his hurts, his misery and his pride.

—6—

Friend or Foe?

For at least a week, Bold confined himself to the same small area in the wood. His activities consisted of sleeping, limping a few yards to grub up some insects or slugs, and burying himself under cover at the slightest sounds of human voices or dogs. The weather was cooling rapidly and there was a distinct nip of frost in the air at night. Bold's leg hurt him less but he knew now that the muscles were damaged irrevocably. He would never again stretch or bend his leg as before. The best he could manage was an accentuated lurch as he moved along while he tried to put as little weight on it as possible. The young fox was beginning to feel very sorry for himself.

The worst of it, to his mind, was the attitude of the

other denizens of the wood. Despite the fact that Bold was now its largest inhabitant, the smaller animals had soon realized he posed no threat at all. So he was exposed to the total disregard of even the weakest of them as they hopped or scurried around his feet. Indeed, they snatched up from before his nose the very insects that he had been reduced to collecting.

Soon, even the insects and snails were hard to find as the temperatures steadily dropped. Bold eagerly ate any berries, bulbs or nuts he could find but, for a large animal, they simply were not a sufficient diet. From time to time he discovered scraps of carrion, but these were few and far between and could not be relied upon. He knew that eventually he must leave the wood to search elsewhere.

Autumn had settled in with a succession of bitterly cold nights, when the young fox was forced at last to make a move. By this time, he had developed his habitual lurching limp into a regular method of locomotion which he adopted automatically as he moved around. Although he no longer thought about it, it made pitiful a comparison with his previous vigorous, supple and tireless lope. He never thought now about live prey and the idea of ever tasting game again was long forgotten. His aspirations rose only to discovering enough invertebrate or vegetable life to sustain himself, while the bonus of a fresh piece of carrion was a treat indeed. This was the existence to which he had been reduced; the robust, confident young cub who had wanted to live in 'the real world'.

But, in spite of it all, Bold never once thought of returning to the protection of the Nature Reserve and the help of his old friends. He had made his choice on leaving the Park. Now there was no going back. He left the wood in the middle of November and at once established a routine of hiding during the day and scavenging for whatever was edible at night. On some occasions, when absolutely nothing could be found, he swallowed mouthfuls of grass, but they usually made him retch.

The scarcity of nourishing food made his already weakened body weaker still. It was as much as he could do to drag himself around and, with little hope of things ever improving for him, Bold began to wonder if it was worth bothering at all. He could never again look forward to the savour of meat, or the thrill of a hunting foray in the crisp, nocturnal air. The effort of lugging his useless leg over a large area in an attempt to find sufficient scraps of food to last until the next night seemed increasingly pointless. So, one night, he just remained in the ditch he used for cover and never stirred at all. Two days and nights passed in the same way. He lay unmoving and uncaring, heedless of the sounds around him. He was quite simply waiting for his end.

On the third day, a warm, sunny, autumn morning revived his flagging spirits and he staggered to his feet. He suddenly thought of the sow badger he had rescued in the coverts and who had pledged to return his good deed. Perhaps she could help him if only he could get to her? He pulled himself out of the ditch, but by now he was so weak that he collapsed in exhaustion with the effort. He cursed himself for not trying to reach her set before when he might have had sufficient strength to do so. He lay panting on the ground until he had recovered a little. Then he tried again. He lurched forward a few metres and collapsed again, his breath coming in hoarse gasps. His poor, wasted body shuddered in the extremity of a final fatigue. He knew he could never make it.

In the air a black bird circled nearby, watching his futile movements. It wheeled to and fro, waiting patiently for the young fox to expire. Finally the fox seemed to lie quite still. The bird coasted down and landed a little distance away. It walked slowly forward.

Bold watched it approach with his one good eye, aware of its intentions. 'You'll . . . have to wait . . . a little longer,' he croaked.

The bird came up to him and examined him critically. Then it uttered a harsh 'caw' of surprise. 'This can't be the bold young fox lying in the dust!' it crowed.

Bold opened his weak eye and blinked as he tried to focus properly. 'So it's you,' he muttered. 'The Carrion Crow of the hawthorn tree.'

'The same. And what's happened to you?'

'I've an injured . . . leg. Can't walk.'

'So you're starving to death?'

'I certainly shall . . . die soon unless . . . help can be brought.'

'Help? For a fox? Who would bring help?' the crow said scornfully.

'One that *I* helped . . . not so long ago.'

'*You* helped? Whom have *you* helped?'

'A sow badger . . . caught in a trap.'

The crow rustled its coal-black wings. 'Well, she doesn't seem in a hurry to remember,' it remarked sarcastically.

'She doesn't know I need her,' Bold wailed miserably. 'If only I . . . could reach her.'

'Too late for that,' said the crow. 'She won't even know of your death.'

Bold tried to raise himself, but sank back again helplessly. A thought passed through his mind. 'I need . . . a messenger,' he gasped.

The crow stared at him in amazement. 'Preposterous!' it exclaimed. 'You haven't the audacity to think that I –'

'I *was* thinking that,' Bold admitted.

'Well! You have some strange notions in your head!
Carry a message for a fox indeed! You must have come
from a strange place with ideas like that. I never heard of
such a thing. And from you – who boasted to me you
could look after yourself!'

'So I did . . . until I got shot.'

'Aha!' the crow cawed triumphantly. 'So the humans
caught up with you, did they? I warned you about them,
but you paid me no heed. You knew better!'

'I was unlucky. I made a mistake,' the young fox
groaned.

'Yes, well, you can't afford mistakes where they're concerned,' answered the bird. 'The way you went around,
puffed up with your own cleverness – I'm surprised you
weren't accounted for long ago.'

'I don't need a lecture,' Bold muttered. 'I've learnt . . .
my lesson. Will you help me or not?'

'Why on earth should I?'

'You were grateful . . . to me once. Remember the
lark's eggs?'

'Absurd animal! You didn't even see them. . . .'

'I haven't got time to argue,' Bold said. 'If you won't
help me . . . I shall die. That's all. *You* can *fly* – how long
would it take you?'

The crow shuffled its feet. 'Where does this badger
hang out?' it asked ungraciously.

'Not far . . . in the pheasant wood . . . the coverts.'

'What?! I'm to fly in there under the nose of a
gamekeeper? Oh yes, and then present myself as a target
for his butcher's collection, I suppose? I'm to risk all that
for *you*? You're mad, my young friend. I thought as
much before.'

'Then you won't do it?'

'Never! What are you to me?'

'Nothing, I admit. But . . . my death . . . will be on your conscience.'

'*I'll* have no conscience!' the bird exclaimed angrily. 'Your pride has brought you to this, nothing else. *I* say you deserve it.'

'Very well,' said Bold. 'Then the cub of the Farthing Wood Fox will die through lack . . . of a friend.' He had fallen back on his last resort. The name and adventures of his father were a legend among the wild creatures for miles around.

The crow looked at him sharply. '*You* his offspring? But wait – it *does* make sense. Your ideals . . . the brotherhood of the Farthing Wood animals . . . . Of course! Now I see it! You come from the Nature Reserve, White Deer Park. So you thought yourself wiser than your parent!'

'Well, I've been . . . proved wrong,' Bold said. 'Now, will you help?'

'I must try,' said the crow in a new tone. 'If it were discovered that I might be responsible for your death in any way, and you related to the one who founded the oath . . . well, it . . . it . . . doesn't bear thinking about.'

'Thank goodness,' said Bold. 'Then go – *please* – hurry!' As the bird leapt into the air and soared aloft, Bold murmured: 'So, Father, even here you still seem to control me.'

It was by now high noon, and the fox knew he could not expect to see the sow badger or any of her tribe until dusk fell. He decided he must make one more attempt to rise and get back to the shelter of the ditch. A fresh danger might threaten his exposed position at any moment. Somehow, with the knowledge that help was at last at hand to buoy him up, Bold managed to stagger to his feet. There he stood for a while, swaying, his wounded leg just brushing the ground. The ditch was only a matter

of a few tottering steps and then he plunged headlong
into it, utterly spent.

He was startled by the sudden reappearance of the
Carrion Crow.

'It's no use searching in the daylight for badgers,' the
bird told him. 'They never appear until the sun
sinks.'

'But that's hours away,' Bold moaned. 'I might not last
that long.'

'Don't worry,' said the crow. 'There is a solution. *I'll*
feed you. I've discovered something really good. We can
share it.'

'What is it?' Bold asked warily, unsure of the bird's pre-
dilections in the nature of food.

'A rabbit carcass.'

'Can you carry it?'

'No, but I can tear pieces off and ferry them
back.'

The crow was being very amenable. Bold was grateful.
'You're very kind,' he said.

'I'll eat some first, shall I, and then bring some for
you?' suggested the bird.

Bold agreed. He was in no position to dispute. The
crow flew away again and was gone a long time. Bold was
beginning to think he had been deserted after all, when
the crow alighted on the edge of the ditch, its bill loaded
with a large piece of dark flesh. This was tossed in Bold's
direction and at once the crow flew off again.

The meat smelled rank, but Bold was desperate and
chewed it with relish. A second piece was soon dropped
to the ditch bottom. The crow returned four more times,
the last time with the biggest chunk of all which it stayed
to see him eat

'That's the last of it,' the bird announced afterwards.

'I'm very obliged to you,' said Bold.

The sun had at last begun to drop behind the horizon. It was time for the crow to renew its search. Bold gave him directions to the quarter of the game wood where lay the badger's set. The bird disappeared.

The food had certainly put new heart into the young fox. He lay, watching the evening shadows fall, with renewed confidence in his own fate. But he hoped his friend the she-badger would be out foraging early or the crow might not find her, for he could not see well enough in complete darkness.

As it was, night had very nearly enveloped the country-side when Bold's messenger returned once more. 'I've located your four-legged friends,' he told the fox. 'They're rushing about collecting what they can for you now. But I'm afraid I can't be of any more assistance to you. I'm a day creature.'

'Of course, I appreciate that,' said Bold. 'I feel a little stronger already, thanks to you. But how will the badgers find me?'

'I really don't know. By scent, I should think. But that's their problem – and yours too.'

'Did you give them *any* indication of my whereabouts?' Bold asked.

'Yes, vaguely.' The crow paused, aware of the fox's mis-givings. 'I'll do one more thing for you,' it said. 'I'll come and find you at dawn, and if they haven't shown up I'll lead them to you. I can't do more.'

'I don't expect it,' replied Bold. 'And I shan't forget this.'

'Very well, then. Till daybreak,' said the bird. Then he was gone, an even blacker shape against the blackness of the night sky.

—7—

A Shadow of Himself

It was a long journey for the badgers to make across open terrain and with their catches in their jaws. There were four of them – the sow badger and three of her progeny, now grown up. Daybreak found them still some distance from their goal, though they *had* been travelling in the right direction. The Carrion Crow spotted them easily and led them towards Bold.

The fox had lain awake most of the night, uttering occasional muffled barks to give a hint of his position. Now he dozed in the ditch, having refreshed himself by licking at the cold dew trapped in the overhanging grass stems.

The crow cawed harshly to waken him, and then, his business done, vanished in pursuit of his own breakfast.

Soon the badgers came clambering into the ditch with their burdens of food. One of them had clawed up some tubers, two of them brought mice, and the sow badger had caught a great rat that had been scavenging by the gibbet. All of the offerings were welcome to the fox, and none of the animals made any noise as he devoured his food piece by piece.

Then the sow badger spoke. 'I scarcely recognize you,' she said.

Bold looked at her, licking his chops. 'My fortunes have dwindled rather since last I saw you,' he replied.

'Perhaps you should have stayed in our wood after all,' she observed.

'Either way I should have fallen foul of the human enemy,' said Bold. 'That gamekeeper was out to get me, and he would have tried another trick.'

'Well, I've seen no traps around since you left,' said the she-badger, 'and I've been very wary, so he must be content with your disappearance.'

'That's why we think that *now* your safest plan is to come back with us,' said one of her offspring, and added: 'You see, the man won't be expecting your return.'

'That's good thinking,' agreed Bold. 'But there's a grave difficulty. I can't travel.'

'Can't you move at all?' asked the sow badger.

'Scarcely. Up till now I haven't eaten for some days, you see. Maybe it might be different now – anyway, I can try.'

'You can take it in stages. We'll bring more food,' she promised. 'Then you can shelter in the set until you've built your strength up.'

'I'm afraid *you're* stranded now, though,' said Bold uncomfortably. 'You can't travel back all that way in broad daylight.'

'We'll find cover and hide up until dusk,' she assured him. 'Then we can all start together.'

Bold told them of the nearby wood where he had hidden himself until recently. 'I'll stay here,' he went on. 'I'll be quite safe – I've been here for days and nothing has been around to disturb me.'

The badgers made themselves scarce. Bold drowsed with a new feeling of hope in his heart. But his faith was ill-founded. He was awakened from his slumbers by a large and muscular dog – a Labrador – who was being exercised in the wood. It smelt the strong odour of fox in the air and gave tongue excitedly. In no time it had galloped up and discovered the luckless Bold cowering in his unprotected lair. Its frenzied barks brought its owner quickly toward the scene. Bold was cornered and completely helpless. His only hope was to feign death for, although this would not fool the dog, the man might be misled. So he lay stiffly on his side in a stark attitude with his tongue lolling from his open mouth, as if he had perished from cold and hunger. The man arrived, quietened the dog, and stood gazing at the animal in the ditch. Bold's heart beat fast. The man prodded him a couple of times with his cane, but each time the fox cleverly rolled back to the self-same position, keeping himself quite rigid. Then the man muttered something to himself and called the Labrador away.

Not until Bold was sure they must be far enough away did he allow himself to stir a muscle. Now it was imperative that he find a safer retreat. He got up and peered cautiously over the top of the ditch. The coast was clear, so out he climbed. He took a few tentative steps. The food had done him some good, for he certainly felt less shaky. He looked around for a place of concealment. There was nothing close enough to hand. Then he remembered that the ditch ran right into the wood to which the badgers had retired. He wondered if he could get that far. Well, at least he would be out of sight as he dragged himself along. There was really no other choice.

The afternoon wore on as Bold limped his way through the mud and dead leaves of the ditch bottom. Of course, he was taking himself further away from his ultimate destination, but that could not be helped. By the time the first trees of the wood closed around him he knew he could go no further and so he sank down where he was. In an hour or two the badgers would be up and around and expecting him to begin another journey. But there was no possibility of that for the present. He must try and keep awake, though; otherwise, they could miss each other.

Through bleary eyes that ached for sleep he at last saw four ghostly-grey shapes moving along under the trees with the badgers' familiar lumbering gait. He yapped to warn them of his presence.

'Why, you've come quite the wrong way!' cried the sow badger. 'Now you've a long trek indeed ahead of you.'

'Had to move – dogs,' muttered Bold. 'Afraid I can't go . . . any further tonight.'

'He's exhausted,' said one of the young badgers unnecessarily.

'*Now* what do we do?' demanded one of the others of its mother.

'I don't know for sure,' she answered. 'This is very awkward.'

'I'm sorry,' groaned Bold. 'But I was lucky to escape.'

'Yes, yes,' she said. 'I understand.' She thought for a moment. 'Well, if you can't be moved, you can't,' she pronounced. 'So I'll have to stay here with you. However, there's no need for all of us to remain behind. You three must go back – now. Four badgers in a wood without a set are too conspicuous. Off with you – and don't stop till you're home.'

'I could try again tomorrow,' Bold offered weakly.

'Yes, well – we'll have to,' said the sow badger. 'Now I must go foraging again.'

The strange wood provided less easy titbits than her familiar one. She brought him a shrew, some bitter bulbs, and a dead toad that had not been quick enough to bury itself away from the first frosts.

'You must eat, too,' Bold remonstrated as she watched over him.

'I managed to dig up a few roots for myself,' she answered unconcernedly. She followed his progress through the meal. 'The crow told me your history,' she informed him.

'My history?' Bold asked. 'Ugh, this toad has an evil taste!'

'Your origins.'

'Oh – the Reserve.'

'I'd never heard of White Deer Park. Of course, the birds know a far wider area of country. But your father –'

'Yes,' sighed the young fox. 'He does seem to be rather well known . . . .'

'Were you perhaps trying to escape from that?' the badger asked him subtly.

'Yes, in a way. But my main idea was to live beyond the confines of the Park. It promised a more exciting existence.'

'Well, you've certainly made up for any lack of excitement in your earlier life,' she remarked. 'But at what cost!'

Bold said, 'For better or worse, it's my life now.'

The following evening the two animals prepared to begin the journey back to the game wood. They had eaten a meal together in companionable silence. Bold had chosen a name for his friend. He called her Shadow because of her constant watch over him. She was amused at the name and seemed rather pleased. They went back through the ditch this time in the opposite direction.

Bold's stamina was still at a low ebb, but he thought he might have sufficient strength to get as far as the gorse patch where he had been lying when the shooting had begun. Their progress was painfully slow.

'I'm relieved that your poor eye has healed,' Shadow had said, 'because you took that knock on my account.' Bold did not tell her that he now realized that his sight had been permanently damaged.

They left the ditch and started across country, Bold hobbling along laboriously. He was very conscious of the fact that his companion was exposing herself to danger because of his slowness. There was almost no real cover until they were amongst the gorse thickets. If daylight should come before they reached them, he must make her run on ahead.

However, they reached shelter without mishap while the darkness held out. For some time during the last stretch of ground Bold had stumbled along blindly, willing his protesting body forward in a sort of haze of exhaustion. When they got amongst the gorse he crashed to the ground like a stone, certain that he could never rise again.

'Bold fox, brave fox,' Shadow murmured compassionately. But he didn't hear her.

They both slept the clock round until the welcome dusk once again folded them in its soft blanket of concealment. Shadow set off as usual in her quest for food. She had not travelled far when she saw, to her astonishment, her three youngsters in the distance apparently on a search. They greeted her delightedly and immediately wanted to know all about Bold.

'It's going to be a longer job than I'd hoped,' she told them.

'We've hidden some food for you a short way back,' said one of the males. 'Where do we bring it to?'

Shadow explained and they trotted off to fetch the supplies. On their return they found their parent running towards them in consternation. 'He's gone!' she cried. 'Bold has disappeared!'

—8—

Alone Again

Bold had watched Shadow set off on her foraging with misgiving. He hated his position of reliance on another. The very thing he had revelled in before – his complete independence – had been completely destroyed. And now, because of his uselessness, he was subjecting another creature to risks he had no right to expect her to share. She – and the crow – had saved him from death. The debt was paid. So, soon after her back was turned, he hauled himself carefully to his feet. His long sleep had refreshed him and he was able to limp out of sight, round the other side of the thickets.

Bold was not sure what to do next. All that he knew was that he would no longer expose Shadow to the danger of being in his company. If possible, he would make his own slow way to the pheasant coverts and the refuge of her set, and if not . . . so be it! His only concern was that she might come looking for him, but he hoped that she would eventually have the sense to make ground to her own home before dawn threatened. He set his immediate sights on reaching the nearest farmed field. This lay on the other side of a hedgerow which formed the border between farmland and the open country. He knew Shadow would never search for him in such a place.

The darkness, at least, obscured his intentions from her as he staggered into the gloom. It was a cold, starlit night without a breath of air and the frosty grass made a crisp whispering noise as he trod it underfoot. The spectral form of a Barn Owl glided over his head on its silent wings. He saw it hover over the hedgerow, then swoop down, pounce, and rise again almost in one uninterrupted movement. So there was food there too! Perhaps he would be lucky enough to kill something *himself* for a change, if he did not set himself too distant a target.

Bold's damaged leg had loosened up slightly during his recent bouts of enforced exercise and he was surprised – and pleased – at the way he managed to keep going. His exhaustion the previous night had largely been due, he decided, to clambering in and out of the ditch. Now he began to hope that he might be over the worst.

As the first faintly perceptible lightening of the sky heralded the end of the night, Bold lurched into the hedgerow. It was made up of a thick band of closely-knit vegetation that was a perfect resting-place, and here he was to have his first piece of good luck for days. He discovered another fox's abandoned earth, and inside it were the remains of numerous catches. Stale and smelly though they were, the famished Bold made a hearty meal. Used to poor fare for so long, it was the closest thing to a feast for him since the last pheasant. So, replete and well content, he gratefully fell into a much-needed sleep.

The next day he awoke before the light had faded and immediately finished off the last few scraps. He left the earth and looked out across a field sown with swede. Here was another food source that he could use in necessity, for the young vegetables were just beginning to thrust themselves out of the soil. Bold's spirits rose considerably. He felt stronger, more hopeful than he had been for a long time. Now, if he could only prove to himself he could still catch his prey – no matter how insignificant – then he really would feel he was on the road to recovery. There would be no need then for Shadow's set or her ministrations.

Bold set himself to explore the hedgerow and its occupants. Songbirds returning to their roosts fluted and warbled amongst the remaining November greenery. There were inviting rustlings amongst the twigs and dead leaves underfoot. A squirrel raced along the top of the shrubbery like a furry goblin, intent on finding a safe perch to enjoy a hazel nut. Bold slunk along with his uneven gait, ears cocked, nose working overtime to identify every new scent. He stopped dead as he spied a vole squatting on a low twig, balancing on its hind legs while it examined some bryony berries. It was at eye level and well within reach. The fox crept forward another couple of centimetres, holding his bad leg out of the way. The vole remained unaware of his presence. Another centimetre. And another. Snap! Bold's jaws caught on the little beast's tail as it leapt for safety. His grip was not good enough and his lunge forward from three legs tilted him off balance. He went sprawling at the hedge bottom and the vole escaped with no more than a painful nip and a fright. Bold rose and shook himself, ashamed of his indignity. Once again, as in the incident with the dormouse, his ability to catch even small prey had been found lacking. The resulting loss of confidence made him unwilling to test his technique again. To be bested by such tiny creatures! It was mortifying to him. He stared across at the field of young swedes. That was to be the limit of his expectations now. For, with a bitterness born of his incapacity, Bold knew he could never again hunt live prey.

He limped out of the hedgerow towards the root crop sown by Man. It was simple to scratch up the ripening tubers and then to fill his belly with the sweetest of them. The added satisfaction that arose from raiding a food supply of the humans made them taste the sweeter. It was Man that had brought him to this low point and he would avenge himself where he could. Suddenly Bold stopped munching and stood motionless. Yes! That was his future now! The humans would be made to pay for his injury. Wherever they stored food or left edibles lying around he, the fox cub Bold, would capitalize upon it. Men would provide him with the food they had deprived him of catching himself.

Sustained by this promising and daring idea, Bold finished his supper and retired to the earth in the hedgerow to mull it over. It was an excellent plan that would require a mixture of caution and courage, he decided. He was no longer in a position to challenge Man by daylight for he had no turn of speed. His movements must therefore be strictly during the dark hours. So when night fell on his meditations, he issued forth for a second raid on the vegetable field.

As he went about his task, feeling more light-hearted now in the new role he had assumed for himself, he became aware of a ghostly shape moving about on the far side of the field. He hobbled hopefully towards it. To his delight he found Shadow the she-badger enjoying the same tasty roots. As he approached she looked up in alarm and prepared for flight.

'Wait!' he called to her. 'It's Bold! Your friend!'

Shadow paused and waited for the fox to come up. 'Alas,' she said, 'we badgers don't have your keen sight, otherwise . . . . But I'm glad to see you!' she finished enthusiastically. 'We'd given you up for lost.'

Bold explained the reason for his disappearance.

'I understand you,' she said quietly. 'But you're too particular. We really wanted to help.'

'I know,' Bold answered. 'But, for me, it's better this way.'

'Then I can't persuade you to come back with me to the set now?'

'No. But thank you. I have another plan.'

Shadow regarded him with interest. 'Do enlighten me,' she urged.

'I'm going to live off the humans,' Bold answered simply.

Shadow's jaws dropped open. 'You mean –'

'I mean whenever and however I can,' he finished for her.

'Well!' Her eyes held admiration. 'So you still intend to live up to your name?'

Bold was pleased with that remark. 'I shall try,' he replied. 'But I shan't take stupid risks.'

'Won't that restrict you?'

'Of course it will,' he said. 'But what does that matter? A beast in my condition can't afford risks except minor ones. From what my father told me of human behaviour, wherever they are in evidence food is there for the picking.'

'But a different sort of food from your preference?' queried Shadow.

'I'm already getting used to that,' he assured her. 'I may

have to adapt further still . . .'

'What about your den?' she asked next.

'I already have one base,' said Bold, looking over his shoulder. 'Over there – in the hedgerow.'

'Underground?'

'Exactly. A very lucky find.'

'You certainly seem well set up,' said Shadow, 'and if you can adapt your diet as you say . . . .'

'If I have to, I will,' Bold said with conviction.

'I respect your determination,' she told him.

Bold enjoyed her flattery. It made it seem he did have a purpose, after all, rather than it being just a question of eking out an existence. 'Well,' he said, 'I suppose I might see you from time to time?'

'Very likely,' she said. 'Or one of my family.'

'Till then, Shadow, my friend,' Bold said brightly.

'Good luck,' she whispered, and they parted.

Bold limped back to the earth, greatly heartened. He felt a keen anticipation for the beginning of his campaign on the morrow.

——9——

A Good Catch

Bold could not sleep for a long time. He was excited by what he felt was a new beginning in his life. The unmistakable sound of human voices pierced his consciousness a couple of times during the day, serving as a pertinent reminder of the challenge he had set himself.

At dusk he awoke from a rather uneasy sleep. He lay a little longer in his den, conserving his strength until the full darkness had spread over the area. Then he emerged into a rainy night. The hedgerow dripped with moisture and the air was filled with a sort of misty dampness. Bold was intoxicated by the myriad scents wafted to him by the quivering leaves and plants. There was an aroma of warm little bodies heightened by the smell of wet fur. But his direction lay elsewhere.

He crossed the vegetable field carefully and without
hurry, this time ignoring its offer of food. He was after
new tastes. He picked up the smell of human spoor and
followed it along a well-worn path. As he had expected, it
led towards a dwelling-place of Man. This was, in fact, a
farmhouse, surrounded by a collection of outhouses.
There was a scent of dog in one quarter which Bold
studiously avoided. He slunk around the wall of a yard,
licking up moisture from a runnel of rainwater as he
crept forwards. On the other side of the cottage, a
pungent odour greeted his eager nostrils. Literally
following his nose, he went to investigate. A gap in the
wall led into an area of mixed plants. Bold was able to tell
by their smell which ones were intended to be used as
food. In one corner there was a sort of mound comprised
of all sorts of odds and ends and it was from there that the
most interesting scents came. There were scraps of vegetable peelings and one or two rather bald-looking bones
among the debris. Bold licked at the bones and
swallowed some of the tastier smelling parings. But there
was nothing very much here. He stole along the side of
the wall for he heard movements under a bushy plant
closer to the house.

A pair of bantams had been allowed to make their nest
in the open and they had been making nervous noises as
Bold betrayed his presence. They scurried away as he
approached and the young fox watched them without
giving chase. He knew they could have run around all
night from one spot to another and *he* would never have a
chance of catching one. But what did interest him were
the three eggs which the hen bird revealed to his view as
she abandoned guard. Bold remembered the Carrion
Crow. Now it was time to sample something which he
had rejected before. First, he sniffed at the strange-
looking objects with great care. They smelt inviting

enough, for the scent of the hen's breast feathers was still attached to them. He took one in his jaws and bit into it. Out poured the contents on to the ground while Bold held a mouthful of unpalatable shell. He licked at the liquid, found it delicious, and made short work of the other two eggs. But his exploration of the cottage garden had to end sooner than he wished. A breeze got up and blew his scent downwind to the farm dog. A frenzy of barking broke out and Bold made as fast an exit as he could, leaving the bantams to return ruefully to the robbed nest. Bold saw no other chance of food nearby so he limped back towards the swede field. His hunger was not entirely satisfied, but the vegetables did not tempt him. Safely back in his earth, he felt reasonably content with the results of his first expedition. But he could not get the thought of those two bantams out of his mind. He knew he had no speed to catch them in a chase, but why couldn't his other innate skill – stealth – serve his purpose, especially as he had found the nesting-place? The more he thought, the more the idea appealed to him and his mouth began to water in anticipation.

Bold decided to pay another visit to the farmhouse garden – but not on the next night. He intended the little pair of fowls to be lulled into a false sense of security. So the next night he hobbled away in another direction to see what he could find. It was a long way to the next human habitation; another farm. By the time he reached its boundaries he was too tired to do much exploring. He was lucky to find another dump of waste, and he contented himself with what edible scraps he could dig out. Now he was in difficulties, for he was too weary to get home. There was no hedgerow here – no cover of any sort, except a few, isolated, large trees which would not hide a fox.

What could he do? He could not be found near the

farm buildings when daylight arrived. But who would look for him *in* one of the buildings, or even think of finding a fox in such a place? There was an open barn well stocked with hay that smelt sweet and warm and inviting. He would be well concealed in the depths of that and, tomorrow night, he would undertake his return journey. Bold was delighted with his own impudence and off he went to the dark barn to bury himself amongst the bales.

During the day there was plenty of activity in and around the farm complex. Cows were milked, animals fed, men went to work and came back. But Bold slept on. The farm cat stood on the threshold of the hay barn and sniffed gingerly at the alien scent, fearing to go further. The sleeping fox was undisturbed. Only the sparrows who flitted to and fro among the rafters knew of his presence and even they deserted the scene when evening came.

Bold roused himself from his fragrant couch. It was time to stir. Two mice killed by the cat still lay at the side of the barn. The well-fed cat had toyed with them but had not deigned to eat them. Bold did. It was the first fresh meat he had tasted since he had left the care of Shadow. He visited the rubbish patch again and found some fat worms wriggling amongst the rotting base of the pile. These and a discarded apple core made Bold's hasty meal before he began his homeward journey.

All the way he thought of nothing but the prospect of the following night. The weather was mild and muggy – the year's last fling of warmth before freezing December was ushered in. Bold crept gratefully into his earth and covered his nose with his brush.

Twenty-four hours later he emerged, feeling brisk and alert for his venture. He reached the nearby farm and began to slink quietly towards the garden. Because of his uneven pace, he had to make particularly strenuous efforts to ensure his silence. All the time he tested the air for sound or smell of the guard dog. His progress was painstaking but uninterrupted. Like a shadow he slid into the garden and slowly neared his target. The heavy cloud layer which made the night so warm added a welcome additional layer of darkness to his endeavours.

Bold froze abruptly as he heard soft, stirring noises about a metre away amongst the shrubbery. Had the birds sensed his approach? Seconds ticked by. Nothing happened. He took another couple of steps. Again the sound of rustling feathers – then quiet. Now Bold trod on the soft soil by the plants, front paws first. He had almost ceased to breathe. His rear leg – the good one – followed. He held himself stiff as he prepared to drag round the damaged leg. Only that could betray him now. Slowly, slowly, he brought it level. It brushed a plant, hardly stirring the foliage. But it was enough. Out rushed the bantams, the hen one way, the cock straight into his waiting jaws and crunch! it was done. Bold stayed no longer than it took for him to immobilize his victim. While the hen bird dashed everywhere in panic, the victorious fox limped his way out of the garden. Now he went more quickly but still he listened for sounds of the dog, his heart beating rapidly. He could hardly believe his luck.

As he neared the field of swede he dropped to his belly suddenly as he saw a badger again rooting amongst the plants. He watched the animal, lying doggo. Yes, it was Shadow. He knew her movements. Jealous of his prize, Bold cursed her appearance on the scene. For if she spotted him, he would have to offer to share his meal. She had worked hard to feed him not so long ago. She seemed in no hurry to move on. Tubers and roots were amongst her favourite provender and, as he knew, the ones in this field were especially succulent. At last, while the cock's warm body grew cold, the sow badger seemed to have garnered all she wanted. Her slow enjoyment of her meal irritated Bold beyond measure. His mouth ran dry with his waiting and all the while she munched the roots with every appearance of relish.

Then, when Bold thought he could stand it no longer, Shadow stopped eating and came straight towards him. Bold dropped the bird and sighed. His frustrating wait seemed to have been for nothing.

'Bold!' she cried gladly. 'I didn't see you before.'

He was on his feet now. 'I – er – I've just come this way,' he replied awkwardly.

Her glance picked out the dead fowl. 'I see you've been busy,' she said, comprehending his predicament at once. 'You needn't worry. I'm quite content. You enjoy your catch.'

'No, no,' Bold protested half-heartedly. 'Share and share alike.'

'Wouldn't dream of it,' she answered. 'You must have worked hard for that.'

Bold relaxed. 'Well, yes, I did, it's true,' he admitted. 'I'm sorry, Shadow. It's just that –'

'No explanation required,' she assured him. 'I understand perfectly. You need all you can get for yourself with your handicap. But you've done well!'

'Thank you,' he said. 'I *was* feeling rather pleased with myself.'

Shadow said: 'I won't delay you any longer. I bet you've been drooling!'

She made her departure and Bold made haste to his den. He took a long time over his meal, anxious to savour each juicy mouthful to the full. It might be many days before he was so successful again. Afterwards he dreamed of the game wood, with himself, perfectly sound of limb, picking off the plumpest pheasants to eat without the least effort. So vivid were these exploits that Bold had some difficulty adjusting to reality when he awoke. So much so, that he was consumed with one ambition: to catch the other bird – the cock bantam's mate.

Evening found him approaching the farm again, with the same caution and silence as before. The cottage loomed ahead of him, slumbering in the soft air. Nothing seemed to stir. Gradually he pulled himself towards the garden, hesitating a little as his senses told him that there had been a change made here – as yet he knew not what. Then, in the gloom, he saw a strange shape where the bantams' nest had been, under the shrubbery. The hen bantam had been securely shut away in a pen for the night – the humans had seen the need for her protection. Bold paused, wondering if it were worth his while to investigate the contraption. He limped a little closer.

Suddenly he was frightened out of his wits. The farm dog had been moved from its usual kennel and tethered as an extra sentry under the back wall of the farmhouse. A great black shape leapt out of the shadows, straining like a panther on a rope, and barking fit to bring the house down. Its gleaming fangs and furious eyes were like a vision in a nightmare. Bold turned tail and fled, his damaged leg bumping over the ground in pursuit of the others. Every moment he expected a crushing body to fall on him, bearing him down and pinning him, helpless, to the ground. But the barks became more distant and he started to breathe freely again.

He did not stop until the sanctuary of his earth was reclaimed. He had had a narrow escape and he vowed never to go near that place again. It was as well he had eaten his fill the previous night, for he got nothing this time. But it seemed the humans were not satisfied with giving Bold a scare. They knew a fox had taken the cock, and that he was ranging the area. While he did so he remained a menace. So they set about eliminating that menace.

The farm dog was put on his track the next morning and, as the track was fresh, it was not difficult to follow. Across the vegetable field came the dog, with young men behind carrying spades, and a terrier. Bold heard them as they breasted the hedgerow. The dog barked triumphantly at his entrance hole. Flight was an impossibility. The large animal was pulled back and Bold heard a scrabbling sound. The terrier had been pushed into his earth. Soon afterwards the hole was stopped, blocking out all light.

Bold stood at bay, ready to snap at the little cur who was growling at him in the darkness, his hackles on end, stiff as a hairbrush. There was another hole leading out of the den and slowly Bold backed towards it, watching the plucky little dog in case of a sudden rush. But his back felt a wall of earth. He was holed up with no escape route and the terrier holding him at bay.

Then he heard men's urgent voices and the sound of their spades striking the surface. The soft moist earth began to drop in on him and the edge of a spade scoured his back fur like a scythe. Daylight filtered into the den while the heavy tools beat away the protective ceiling of mould. In a terrifying upheaval of soil, the cowering body of Bold was exposed to the open air like a defence-less grub in its tunnel. The large farm dog, its fury unabated, cracked the peace of the countryside with its deafening roar. The terrier was hauled out of the pit and Bold cringed, waiting for the cruel thud of a spade across his body that would spell his doom. His bad leg collapsed under him and he sprawled on his stomach. His adventures were over.

—10—
Not Guilty

The two young men looked down at the puny, maimed beast quailing at bay. They glanced at each other with raised eyebrows. Was this poor specimen the fox that had killed the bantam cock?

'*He* can't be the culprit,' one observed to the other.

'Must have a mate who did the job,' muttered his companion. 'You can see the feathers clear enough.'

'Quiet, Punch! Stop that row!' yelled the first man to the large dog. It ceased to bark and began to whine and growl exasperatedly in a frustrated manner. The terrier went on yapping shrilly.

'We'd better leave this poor brute,' said the second

man. '*He's* no threat to us. Doubt if he'll see the winter through.'

'Not him, with that injury. And his mate won't stay in these parts now she's got no cover.'

'She might have another earth, though?'

'I don't know of one,' said the man who was holding the terrier. 'But we'd best keep our eyes peeled.'

Bold, awaiting the awful final moment, saw through glazed but astonished eyes, the men turn on their heels and stump away across the field, taking their tools and dogs with them. He scrambled out of the wreckage of his den and pushed his way through the hedgerow to the other side and on into open country as fast as his poor gait allowed. Every second he expected to be pursued. But he limped on, each laboured step taking him further away from danger. No sound came from behind. At last he realized he was not going to be followed and paused to give himself a vigorous shake, freeing his coat from its shower of mould. The ways of men were indeed incomprehensible.

Bold's only thought now was to get as far away from the area as he could before disaster should overtake him again. Fear lent him a new strength and, by late afternoon, he felt he had come a long way. He was in country he had not seen before and now he knew he must rest. His whole body trembled as a result of his exertions, while his legs ached abominably. He staggered into a stand of young holly on the edge of a spinney and fell, rather than lay down, on the carpet of dead leaves underneath, quite oblivious of their spines.

Unknown to Bold, a familiar, black shape was coasting on air currents in the winter sky, occasionally flapping its wings as it lost height. Satisfied that the exhausted fox would be unable to stir for some hours, it flew away over the tree-tops uttering its harsh cries in a sleepy manner as the daylight failed.

Bold was roused at sun-up by a chill wind ruffling his fur. The ground all around the spinney was stiff with frost. Even the edges of the holly leaves had a coating of white. Bold shivered and peered out at a world made silent by thick eddies of mist. Then he blinked in disbelief as he saw a large black bird stepping out of the fog, its bill stuffed with pieces of dark meat.

The Carrion Crow dropped his burden by the fox and croaked a welcome. 'On the move again, I see?' he added, 'then you'll be needing this.'

Bold saw the pieces of stale, raw meat more closely. 'Timely indeed,' he remarked. 'I haven't eaten for two days, and so I appreciate it more than you know.' He took a gulp. 'This *is* good,' he said. 'But where did you find it?'

'Oh-ho! There's plenty more of that if you know where to look,' chortled the crow.

'And where would that be?' Bold asked eagerly.

'In the town.'

'Town?' Bold ate another piece of meat.

'Yes – not far from here. Full of humans and their buildings – *and* their food!'

Bold's ears pricked up. 'What sort of cover is there?' he wanted to know.

'Oh, plenty round about. You'd have to stay on the fringe, of course, and make raids at night.'

'That's rather what I had in mind,' Bold said wryly.

'Sorry. Don't need to teach you your craft, I'm sure,' the crow answered quickly.

'How long would it take me to get there?' Bold asked next.

The crow said: 'I don't know. I can only judge distances as a bird flies. It may be a whole night's travelling time on four legs.'

'Or, in my case, three,' Bold reminded him sardonically. 'Then I'd better start at nightfall.' He finished the meat the crow had brought him. 'What direction must I take?'

'Watch me,' said the crow and took to the air. Bold followed his flight until he became a mere dot in the sky. The bird did not return but Bold knew all he wanted to know. He got up and stretched his three sound limbs. He felt stiff, sore and chilled to the marrow. He needed to get some warmth back into his body, and the only way to do that was to keep on the move. The freezing mist set his weak eye watering, but its enveloping coils were also his friend. No prying observer could see the hobbling fox's feeble attempts to run, and for that Bold was very glad.

A thin sun touched the shrouded countryside but failed to penetrate. Only the wind succeeded in tossing the swirling vapour about like patches of damp fleece. The young fox's blood ran more quickly through his veins as he pattered here and there, whiling away the time to when the sun should finally surrender its fight.

Darkness came early and Bold set his course for his new objective, following the bearing of the crow's flight. He travelled warily and at an easy pace. The wind had dropped and the air was very still. Scarcely a murmur reached Bold's ears from the creatures of the night. After some time he became aware of a faint gleam which seemed to lie on the distant horizon. It grew steadily more bright as he drew nearer. Though he did not know it, it was the lights of the town.

Eventually Bold began to look for shelter. He did not

know how far he had come but, as usual, his legs told him it was time to rest. He hid himself away in the nearest piece of woodland, content with his progress for that night. The next evening he was off again in the direction of that illumined piece of sky. The mist had disappeared and presently he heard quite plainly the muffled sounds of the town. They were, as yet, too distant to be alarming. He had no experience of the terrifying noises that humans can make in their daily lives. Motor traffic and the blare of machinery were beyond his knowledge. The crow had not warned him what to expect and, at the end of his second night's travelling, he rested quite unprepared for the shock that was to come with the morning.

He had arrived on the edges of some playing fields where a litter basket had provided him with some miscellaneous pickings. It had been easy to overturn it to get at the contents and, after he had eaten, Bold laid himself down at the bottom of a privet hedge. When dawn broke, the first noises of a wakening town were carried to the sleeping fox, dispelling his slumbers. Wrapped in his thick, winter brush he lay without moving, but now wide awake. The early morning din was as nothing to what would happen when the town's pulse really began to beat. Bold was uneasy. He moved from the hedge to find thicker cover. There wasn't any. He began to panic. The noise was growing steadily louder. He couldn't keep still. Every fresh roar made him turn in fright, but he was limping around in circles. Suddenly he saw what looked like a dark hole and made straight for it. It was a small hut, containing some tools belonging to the groundsman of the playing fields. The door had been left ajar and Bold blundered in, upsetting the stacked implements and sending them crashing to the wooden floor. Now quite terrified, he tottered out again, casting about wildly for anything that might shelter him. He saw some people walking nearby with their dogs and slunk back to the privet hedge. But the din seemed to fill the air, blotting out his ability to employ even his most basic instincts. At last he heard a muttered croak close at hand.

'Come with me. I'll show you where.' The Carrion Crow was waiting for him, perched very conspicuously in a rowan tree. He took off and flew low, directly across the playing fields. Bold stumbled after him mindlessly. On the other side the bird waited for him to catch up and then flew straight to a patch of waste ground, which was choked with bramble, elm-scrub and thick banks of rusty-leaved weeds. Bold needed no bidding to dive into this mass of vegetation until he was quite invisible. The crow sat on the top of a sycamore sapling and spied out the land.

'You're quite safe now,' he said.

Bold refrained from answering. The last half hour, particularly the crossing of the playing fields in full view, had quite unnerved him.

'You took longer to get here than I was expecting,' the crow went on.

Now Bold said: 'I wish I hadn't come. That dreadful noise! I've never heard anything like it before. I'd have been better off staying where I was.'

'Nonsense!' scoffed the crow. 'No good being safe and secure elsewhere if you can't find anything to eat.'

'I was doing all right,' Bold muttered from the undergrowth.

'You'll do better here,' the crow told him, 'when you've adjusted yourself.'

'That I shall never do.'

'You know, noise itself can't harm you. It is town noise made by humans, and no danger whatsoever to you or any other creature. You simply have to get used to it. It's the same every day. At night, when you'll be around, it's quieter. All you've got to watch out for are the *makers* of the noise.'

Bold had calmed down a little by now. The din had not increased and there was no sign of it approaching nearer to him. It *would* be worth waiting until nightfall to see if the crow's words were correct.

'You'll soon change your mind about things once you start foraging,' the bird reassured him. 'There are rich pickings if you know where to look for them.'

'Very well,' said Bold. 'I shall give it a try. And, by the way, I forgot to thank you for your rescue operation.'

'I have to confess to some self-interest in this,' said the bird honestly. 'You'll be able to tap sources of food I can't reach. So I'm hoping that my diet might be enriched too. . . .'

'I understand you,' said Bold. 'And I certainly owe you a lot. You shall share anything I find – as long as there's sufficient for me.'

'Naturally. And I will do the same for you – for I shall be about in the daytime. So, between us, we can work this patch for all it's worth. No better place in the winter than close to Man's nesting sites.'

Bold was amused at the other's tone. It seemed his own idea of exploiting the humans was now shared by this bird.

'In fact,' the crow declared, 'it's time I rustled up something now. You stay put,' he added as he left, an unnecessary remark as far as Bold was concerned, who immediately fell asleep.

He was still asleep when his partner returned. The crow searched for a sign of him with his beady eyes but to no avail, so good was the fox's camouflage. Presently he cawed irritably.

'You're back,' Bold mumbled drowsily. Only a slight

rustling of the undergrowth betrayed his whereabouts.

The crow waited patiently but Bold didn't stir. 'Aren't you going to see what I've brought?' he croaked. 'It's all yours. I've eaten my fill.'

Bold crept out from his screen and sniffed at the strange-looking object that awaited him – a packet of sandwiches. He sniffed all round it and gave it a tentative lick. 'What's this?' he asked, looking puzzled.

'Man food,' answered the crow. 'I found it on the ground. It's quite palatable.'

'It smells tasty enough but –' Bold broke off to have another look at it. Then he clawed at the paper wrapping. *That* didn't appear to be palatable.

'You have to accept what comes,' the crow explained. 'Can't afford to overlook *anything*. You'll be surprised what you can eat when you get into the habit.'

Bold had never seen bread before, but there was meat inside it and he found himself eating the whole concoction and enjoying it.

'Was this your meal too?' he asked afterwards.

'No,' said the crow. 'I found some food left out for a cat or dog and ate all that.'

'Some poor creature will go hungry then,' Bold opined. 'I think I shall call you "Robber".'

'Don't waste any sympathy on them,' the crow retorted. 'Those that Man feeds never go hungry. So you and I have every right to take what we can.'

'Yes, Robber,' said Bold drily.

'Yes, Bold,' replied Robber.

—11—

The Urban Fox

When night fell, it was Bold's turn to make a foray. Robber had gone to roost in a secluded place at the top of a tall tree, leaving the young fox to gather his courage together. For a long time the noise from the town continued unabated. But as the nocturnal hours marched by, a comparative peace descended, only occasionally interrupted by a sudden, strident sound. Then Bold was ready to move.

He went limping across the fields, now bathed by a fitful moonlight, and made for the black shapes of the human's dwellings. He paused often to test the air as he went. His powerful sense of smell detected a host of strange scents, none of which was familiar to him. But he pressed on, prepared to take cover only if the smell of dog or that of Man himself was recognizable. The first group of buildings he came to lay in complete darkness. Walls or fences bounded them and their plots of land, and Bold skulked along these barriers like a shadow, searching for an opening. For, unlike other animals of his kind, he could not jump. He soon realized he was indeed handicapped for he was thus effectively debarred from entering most of the gardens. Of course he was able to contort himself wonderfully to slink through the slightest gap; he could flatten himself to scramble underneath an obstacle; he could even dig; but any sort of leap was absolutely beyond his scope.

On that first exploratory roam around Bold succeeded in visiting a number of yards and gardens and this was when he discovered what was to be the mainstay of his food supply for weeks to come – the dustbin. Once he had got used to the clang that some of them made what a remarkable collection of unwanted scraps he found in these receptacles! There was always something, it seemed, of which use could be made. It was almost as if the improvident humans had attempted to encourage him to feast upon these puzzling little dumps of food. Bold accepted each and every thing gratefully as he came to realize that his survival appeared to be ensured. Winter would not claim him as a victim after all.

His inquisitiveness kept him so busy that he forgot how far he was from his new hideaway. Dawn was stealing across the sky as he hastily set off on the return journey. He did not remember his duty to Robber, for he went empty-jawed. Back along the human paths he hobbled until he reached the playing fields. The noise had started up again as he made haste across the wide open space. Only when he reached the waste plot did he realize he had not kept to his bargain.

Robber arrived at the spot, intending to leave Bold to

snooze peacefully. He waddled along the ground, jerkily turning his head this way and that as he searched for the delicacy he was sure the fox would have brought him. Of course, there was none. Robber wondered if Bold had not returned. He flew up to a branch and spied out the land. No sign of any animal. Then he 'cawed' three or four times loudly and harshly with annoyance.

'I'm here,' Bold owned up.

'Ah, now I see you,' said the crow. 'Were you unsuccessful?'

'Er – no, not exactly,' Bold replied awkwardly.

There was a pause. 'Oh! So our bargain is to be a one-sided sort, is it?' remarked the crow.

'Not at all,' Bold hastened to explain. 'I – I was caught rather far from home when dawn broke.'

'I see. Well, as you are still in my debt I shall not be expected to find *you* anything now?'

'Of course not,' said Bold in a small voice.

Robber flew away immediately, without another word. Bold did feel a little shamed and decided he would make up for his failure on his next trip.

The next evening came round wonderfully quickly. December arrived with a stinging squall of sleet that drove across the open fields in a spray of ice-needles. The fox's eyes smarted as he battled against the blast, cursing the handicap of his limp. But there was shelter amongst Man's buildings and Bold again began to enjoy his exploring. In one yard he found two bowls, one containing milk; the other fish. He greatly appreciated the thought-fulness of the humans who had supplied them. There didn't seem to be any other animals nearby to claim the bowls' contents.

He went on cautiously, snapping up pieces of bread missed by birds in one garden, knocking over bins in another to raid the pungent-smelling collections that

spilled from them. He had learnt to retire quickly behind
a plant or other screen as the bin crashed down; then, if
nothing happened after a few minutes, he slunk back to
select his pickings. Sometimes the clattering he caused
did bring a human into the open. On those occasions,
Bold was out of the garden and well away from the scene
before he could be noticed.

On this evening he was to find that there were com-
petitors for his food. He was looking into a large fenced
area of lawn and flower beds behind an imposing house.
The sleet fell slantwise across the grass in a sort of mist.
Out of the shadows around the building there trotted a
brisk, confident-looking fox that seemed to know exactly
what it was about. Bold's muscles tautened as he
watched. The animal stepped lightly across the grass with
a fluid grace that was a perfect illustration of health and
vitality. It made straight for a stone bird-table, the flat top
of which was nearly two metres from the ground. With
the most enviable agility the fox leapt in one flowing
movement up to the top. There it stood, fearlessly survey-
ing its surroundings, before snatching up the remnants
of the birds' leavings. Bold was entranced. He knew it to
be a female, and he was as full of admiration for her
strength as for her grace and elegance. He thought of his
own poor frame; his hobbling walk; his inability to jump,
and he shrank back timidly to avoid being detected.

As luck would have it, after making a brief circuit of the
garden, the vixen came straight towards Bold. Instinctively he flattened himself against the ground. She leapt
the fence effortlessly and landed about three metres from
him. Some slight involuntary movement on Bold's part
betrayed his presence. She turned and looked at him
calmly. No trace of surprise or curiosity was shown by
her. For a few moments they stared into each others'
eyes, then she swung round and trotted coolly away as if

he had been of no more interest than a piece of wood.

Bold felt humiliated by her disregard. Although there was no reason for her to pay him any attention, her nonchalance only made him all the more conscious of his poor appearance. He felt that her reaction might have been quite different had she seen him as he had once been in those first glorious weeks after he had left the Nature Reserve. Now he was indeed quite another animal. His physical deficiencies assumed a new proportion in his mind and his confidence fell to a low ebb. What a cringing, struggling scrap of a creature he had become! He crawled away from the fence, his brush hanging lifelessly between his legs. Why continue the fight? He would be better off out of it all.

But life had to go on and Bold had to go on. He pulled a meaty-looking bone from the next container he upset and began his slow, sad, homeward journey. At least Robber would have no cause for complaint this time.

The crow was delighted with Bold's offering and spent a long time pulling and pecking at the fragments of meat that still clung around the bone. Bold slept deeply, utterly dispirited and tired out by his feelings. Robber came back during the day and dropped a share of his kill for the fox to enjoy, for he did not live entirely off carrion. But Bold made no attempt to fetch it. Flying overhead later Robber noticed the untasted morsel and down he came to reclaim it.

'Shame to waste it if it's not to your taste,' he remarked.

'Have it by all means,' said Bold disinterestedly.

Something in his tone made the bird pause. 'Is there anything wrong?' he inquired.

'Of course – everything's wrong,' Bold growled bitterly.

'Everything?'

'Everything with *me*.'

'Aha!' said Robber. 'So that's it. Feeling sorry for yourself. Doesn't do any good, you know.'

Bold held his tongue.

'You're still alive, Bold, my friend,' the bird went on. 'You would have died out there if you hadn't followed my advice.'

'Might have been the best thing,' Bold muttered. 'After all, what am I doing? Just prolonging the agony!'

'Your leg may not always be so bad,' said Robber encouragingly.

'Yes, it will,' said Bold. 'I shall never run or jump again as I used to do. If anything, it's worse than before.'

'You're not very easy to comfort,' said Robber shortly. 'I don't know why I'm bothering.'

'I'm sorry,' said Bold. 'I ought to be grateful for a comrade, I know. But I think I'm beginning to miss my own kind.'

'That's easily solved,' Robber told him. 'There are plenty more foxes around here.'

'I know, I saw one,' said Bold morosely.

Robber looked at him, his head on one side. 'Couldn't have been a vixen, I suppose?' he chuckled.

'Yes, yes – a vixen,' Bold answered.

'Well, that's hopeful, then?'

'Quite the reverse,' the fox said. 'I'm not the most impressive of beasts, Robber.'

'Oh dear. Now, now,' Robber said awkwardly. 'Humph! Well, you'll soon put some meat back on your bones, *I'm* sure.' He eyed the morsel of food with an air of irresolution, for he badly wanted to eat it. Then he seemed to make a decision. He stepped away from it and turned his back. 'Of course, you won't if you let good food go begging,' he said. 'If you don't hurry and eat what I brought you while my back's turned *I* shall eat it.'

Bold saw the sense in the remark and knew the bird was making a real sacrifice, something almost unknown in the crow family except at nesting time. He came out of hiding and gulped down the food, before Robber could change his mind.

'That's better,' said the crow, as he turned back, but Bold thought he detected a note of disappointment in the familiar croak.

'Thank you, Robber,' he said humbly. 'I'm glad you're my friend.'

The crow rustled his wings and started to preen himself as a diversion. He was just a little embarrassed. 'Well,' he said eventually, 'I wish you good hunting tonight.'

Bold wasn't thinking of his hunting. His thoughts were of a certain lithe young vixen and his one hope was that he might encounter her again.

—12—
Whisper

For the next week Bold visited the same large garden where he had seen the vixen. He couldn't get inside it since he was unable to jump the fence. So, each night, he gazed through the palings in a forlorn way, longing for a glimpse of her. Yet she was never there – at any rate, not at the time he was. Bold became more and more disconsolate. He never mentioned her again to Robber, but the wily crow knew how the wind blew in that quarter. Of course he refrained from saying anything.

Then one evening Bold thought he spotted her. There was certainly an animal moving around at the far end of the garden, shadow-like in the gloom. Bold stared into the darkness until his weak eye ached. He sniffed the air for a clue, but the creature was downwind and he could not catch the scent. If only he could jump! Bold actually snarled in his aggravation. Then he remembered he could still dig.

He began to scrape at the soil in which the fence was sunk. It was quite soft and so he dug in earnest. Every now and again he paused to see if the animal had come any closer. Deeper and deeper went Bold's tunnel, but still he could not seem to reach the bottom of the palings. Then he stopped digging, for the animal in the garden had come out into the open. It was the vixen, and she was approaching the bird-table to repeat her former trick. Bold resumed his digging.

So determined was he to get under the fence that he would have failed to notice the vixen leaping over it, if he had not aroused her curiosity.

'Can you not jump?'

Bold started and looked up. The vixen was poised on the other side of the palings, ready to spring. Bold saw the tightened muscles in her powerful limbs. He felt ashamed of his damaged leg and tried to hide it by tucking it under his body. The vixen leapt the fence.

'Er – no,' Bold muttered. 'No, I can't jump.'

'Are you hurt?'

Bold looked down, unable to meet her penetrating glance. 'I – I was injured – er – a long time ago,' he said, scarcely audibly.

'Unfortunate,' she commented. 'I should save yourself the trouble, anyway. There's very little worth foraging for, in there. Why are you so desperate to get in?'

Bold was taken aback. 'I– er – well, I wanted to – er – I was really trying to dig,' he spluttered.

'Yes, I can see that,' said the vixen, looking at him curiously. 'But what's so important about *that* garden?'

'Nothing, now,' Bold said in a not-at-all bold voice.

The vixen sat down. 'I think you were trying to get to *me*,' she said quietly.

Bold remained silent.

'I haven't seen you before,' she went on. 'Are you new in the area?'

Bold didn't remind her that she *had* seen him before. 'Yes,' he said. 'I moved in from the country when food became scarce.'

'Very wise,' she replied. 'I come around here quite often in the winter to supplement what would otherwise be a rather frugal diet. But for you, things must be doubly difficult.'

'What do you mean?' Bold asked defensively.

'Why, if you can't jump – you can't run, I suppose?' said the vixen.

'No, I can't,' he snapped. 'And nor could you, if you'd been shot in the leg.'

'My, my, aren't you touchy?' she said. 'Accidents will happen. Why are you so sensitive about it?'

Bold said nothing.

'If I were you, I'd be glad I'd survived,' the vixen went on. 'How did it happen?'

Bold explained the circumstances. The vixen listened with evident sympathy. 'Bad luck indeed,' she said seriously. 'Maybe those humans were avenging themselves on you for stealing the pheasants *they* wanted to kill.'

Bold thought this a shrewd observation. He thought for a moment. 'I've escaped death twice at their hands,' he said. 'Now it would be ironic indeed if I survived to an old age by living on their leavings.'

'But a sort of justice,' commented the vixen.

Bold pulled himself out of the hole and shook his coat energetically. It wasn't until he took a few steps that the vixen realized just how serious his injury was. Something moved within her. 'If you'd accept help, I'd be glad to give it,' she told him. '*I* could be your legs.'

Bold winced internally. His pride took another blow. 'I'm not quite helpless yet,' he replied testily. 'But I thank you for your offer,' he added in a more gracious manner.

The vixen realized she had touched him on a raw spot. She thought she had better leave him to his own devices. 'Farewell, then,' she said quickly. 'And good luck.'

Bold almost called her back. But again pride got in the way. He watched her supple young body slip away into the darkness and sighed. How he wished she could have seen him when he had been better favoured!

Quite mechanically he set about finding his supper, his thoughts still full of the meeting he had sought for days. He ate without appetite and took more care over choosing a titbit for Robber than he did for his own meal. He returned home early, full of a sense of regret.

Bold never saw the vixen in the garden again. But the two of them were destined to meet again in different surroundings. About a month after their last encounter, in the middle of winter, Bold was crossing the playing fields now covered by the first fall of snow. An intake of kitchen leavings combined with the exclusion of any fresh meat from his diet, had wrought its change in the fox's appearance. He was thinner than ever and his coat mirrored the lack of really nutritious food. The severe cold heightened the stiffness of his old wound and in every way he looked like an animal who was struggling to hold the threads of its life together. Unknown to Bold, his faltering steps through the snow were witnessed by the vixen, who herself was finding the going more tough. But she had no thought for her own problems as she watched his progress.

The vixen's heart melted at the sight of him and she

was filled with compassion. A few seconds longer she watched; then she hastened after him and, with a few bounds, drew alongside.

Bold turned an astonished glance on her. 'Well,' he said, 'how goes it with you?'

'Rather better than with you, I would think,' she said softly. 'I – I – want to help – or – I want to *hunt* with you,' she corrected herself.

Bold noticed the slip but he felt he couldn't refuse her offer again – nor, indeed, did he want to. It seemed that, since his injury, he was fated to be helped by other creatures. His dreams of independence had turned sour. Yet, despite that, the prospect of the company of this young vixen caused a flicker of excitement inside him.

'I should be glad of your company,' he said diplomatically. 'We might bring each other luck.'

They reached the cover of the first buildings and the vixen stopped. 'Let's not go sniffing for scraps,' she suggested. 'I've discovered a place by the side of some water where there's a colony of rats. But we have to go farther into the town. What do you think?'

Bold began to drool at the idea of eating fresh meat again. 'Lead the way,' he said with bravado.

The vixen looked at him for a moment as if to make certain of his true feelings. Bold licked his lips. 'Very well then,' she said and led off.

Only now did Bold appreciate to the full her skill in hunting. She was so light-footed as to be noiseless; she followed unerringly the path of the thickest shadows, and when it was necessary to cross an open space she skimmed across it on her silken feet like a zephyr. Bold lumbered after her, feeling himself to be like a chain around her dainty legs, impeding her swiftness. She paused regularly to allow him to catch up. Neither spoke a word, but Bold's eyes told her all. Eventually the gleam of water could be seen ahead, where it bathed itself in moonlight. The vixen seemed to melt into the darkness as she crept cautiously forward. Bold limped behind as quietly as he could, maintaining a discreet distance.

'There!' she hissed to him. 'But wait – the water is higher now.' She scanned its edge. 'Yes, the colony is still there, but the water surrounds them now. They've become an island.'

Bold peered over her flank. He was looking at a canal and its still, night-black water. Close to the bank a mound of debris, mud and vegetation was situated, and the beasts who favoured this site as their home were scuttling around it, some squeaking aggressively at others – perhaps at rivals.

'The water level has risen,' said the vixen. 'That makes it easier, because their retreat is cut off.'

'But you'll have to swim?' Bold asked.

'Of course. But that's simple enough, if you don't mind the cold.'

'*I* can't swim,' said Bold hurriedly, 'with only three useful legs.'

'I didn't expect you to,' replied his companion. 'I'll bring enough for both.' She moved to the edge of the bank and let her body sink into the icy water. Only her head showed above the surface as she paddled towards her victims, the ripples streaming back from her shoulders. Now the rats heard her and pandemonium ensued on their little island. The squeaks became shrieks and they dashed about, colliding with each other, and running this way and that in their terrified indecision. The next moment the female fox pulled herself from the canal and crashed amongst them, snapping to left and right as the rats scattered. Some of them leapt into the water to escape the slaughter and began to strike out for the bank.

Bold lay doggo, his muzzle protruding just an inch or two over the grassy edge. None of the escaping animals could suspect that there was another fox awaiting their arrival on land. As they tried to scramble clear of the canal, Bold felled the first two before those behind saw what fate awaited them. But some of the others hastily paddled further downstream and evaded their certain death.

The vixen started to carry her prey back to land. Soon she and Bold were contemplating the results of their night's work.

'You're a wily hunter,' Bold commented with satisfaction.

'You played your part too,' she answered hastily. 'We've more than enough here.'

'Light as a whisper,' he murmured to himself. 'And so I shall call you.'

'Whisper? Then I must have a name for you.'

'I am called Bold,' he said, 'and bold I was. I wish you had known me then.'

'I too,' said Whisper. 'Well, Bold – let's eat.'

They took as much as they wanted and ate in a dark, concealed spot without fear of interruption.

'Tomorrow we can come back for the rest,' said Bold. 'We must hide our catch away.'

This they did, and covered it with earth and twigs. But Bold kept one of the rats back.

'Haven't you had enough then?' Whisper asked him with surprise.

'It's not for me,' he explained.

'Then for whom?'

'Robber – the crow.'

'*Crow?*' she echoed. 'How absurd.'

'No, not absurd,' Bold said patiently. 'We have a

bargain between us. He brings me food – and I him. He kept me alive on more than one occasion.'

'Well, this is strange,' said Whisper uncomprehendingly. 'But I didn't go rat-catching for the sake of a bird.'

'Then it is one *I* caught,' said Bold pointedly.

'Indeed.' She stared at him. 'But your unusual arrangement can end now. You have no need of such an ally any longer.'

Bold held his tongue. He was not prepared to dispute the case. Robber was his friend and he had no intention of deserting him. It seemed that Whisper might be a little jealous.

There came the point on their return journey when their ways lay in different directions.

'Where do you sleep?' Whisper wanted to know.

Bold explained. 'It's perfectly safe,' he added. 'And you?'

'I have an earth,' she answered. 'You would be safer still there.'

'I'm most grateful, Whisper,' he said. 'But tonight I must return to my usual place. Robber will be looking for his titbit at daybreak.'

'Please yourself,' she said shortly. 'I'll be at the waterside tomorrow night.'

'And so will I,' said Bold.

—13—
The Changes of a Season

Robber was delighted and amazed with Bold's present and croaked a harsh little song to himself in his pleasure. 'Things are looking up, Bold, my young friend,' he said afterwards. 'You're a hunter again!'

Bold had to deny his prowess. 'I had help,' he said.

'Oh-ho. It isn't a certain young – er –'

'Yes, yes,' Bold cut in good-humouredly. 'A young female. After today you won't see me here, Robber. She has her own den – with room for me.'

'Well, well, that *is* good news,' remarked Robber. 'Er – I suppose you'll still be hereabouts, will you? I shall stay on till the spring.'

'Oh, yes. Hereabouts,' Bold assented. 'From now on I'll leave you your share of the catch under the privet hedge.'

'Oh, no!' said the crow. 'Forget about me. No need to worry. *I* can manage. You'll have other things to do now.'

'Well, if you want to see me, or need me for anything,' said Bold, 'leave a message under the hedge. Do you follow me?'

'I do indeed, my friend. And you will do likewise?'

'I most certainly will.'

'Good. Then that's settled,' said Robber, 'and very amicably too. And now for that rat.'

The next night Bold and Whisper unearthed their cache of food by the canal and enjoyed their second meal together. This time Bold did not reserve a portion for the crow, and the pair of foxes demolished the remainder of their catch. Whisper was quick to notice this point and the significance of it was not lost upon her.

'You'll be returning with me to my den?' she asked her companion.

'Yes, I shall,' Bold answered diffidently.

'You'll find it a deal more comfortable than sleeping above ground – and warmer too,' she remarked.

They went together to the canal bank to lap at the inky water. There was no sign of activity on the rats' island. It seemed those that had escaped the foxes' hungry jaws had deserted the site. Whisper led Bold away from the canal and along different paths towards the other side of the town. They came to a large churchyard enclosed by an old stone wall. Now they were suddenly faced with a problem, since Whisper's earth lay within this boundary and she had been accustomed to jump the wall at a low point to reach it.

'There must be another way in?' Bold asked her hopefully.

'I don't think so. I completely forgot about your difficulty in jumping. Oh, Bold, what a stupid creature I am! But we're not beaten yet.'

'Of course we're not. You know I can dig.'

'It may be the only way; but let me do a bit of reconnoitring.'

She left him lying, rather too conspicuously for his liking, against the wall where a growth of ivy provided only a scant cover. After making a quick circuit, she came back.

'I think I've found the answer,' said Whisper. 'Follow me.'

She took Bold to a spot where the stones of the ancient wall had started to crumble. She began to scratch at the falling blocks with a backward, kicking motion, and succeeded in making a small hole in the stonework.

'Only big enough for a weasel to get through,' Bold muttered unhelpfully.

'Be patient,' said Whisper and recommenced scratching at the surrounding stones with her front paws. The wall continued to crumble and the hole grew gradually in size. Whisper paused, panting with the effort.

'My turn now,' said Bold and scrabbled vigorously with his claws until the hole was large enough to push his head through. 'Only a little more, I think,' he said, and soon he could slip his body through so that the hairs of his coat just brushed the sides. Whisper followed him. She trotted through the tombstones, this way and that, until, under the lee of the wall on the far side of the churchyard, she reached the entrance to her earth.

Bold looked at it. 'It's well concealed,' he observed. There was thick ground-ivy, and piles of dead leaves that had fallen from an overhanging horse-chestnut lay all around. 'How did you find it?' He followed her inside.

'Oh, in the course of my travels,' she told him.

It was a few degrees warmer inside the earth than the outside air. To a fox that meant everything. Bold stretched himself luxuriously. The smell of the vixen was strong, along with the usual musty dampness of an underground home.

'Are you tired?' Whisper asked.

'Yes,' Bold replied. 'And content.'

'I'm glad about that,' she said. 'I think you've found life very hard recently?'

'I have,' Bold admitted. 'I didn't expect to find Death staring me in the face quite so soon.'

Whisper pondered awhile. 'You must have seen several winters, I suppose?' she murmured drowsily.

Bold, already half-asleep, thought he had misheard. 'What did you say?'

'Oh, I was only wondering about your life before you got hurt,' she said. 'Did you range far over the seasons?'

Now Bold sat up. 'You mistake me,' he said. 'I've yet to survive my first winter.' He was most indignant.

Whisper's mouth dropped open. She was stunned. 'But – but,' she stammered. 'Can this be true? I am –'

'It's certainly true,' Bold snapped. 'I opened my eyes for the first time last spring.'

'You must forgive me,' Whisper answered. 'I had no idea. You seem so . . . . But you're not much more than a cub then? I myself am a season older!'

'This is your *second* winter?' Bold asked. Now he was surprised, though he didn't really know why.

'Indeed it is. You see, I thought . . . . Of course, your injury . . . .' she broke off in embarrassment.

'I hadn't realized I'd aged quite so much,' Bold remarked sourly. He was quite taken aback by the revelation. What *had* happened to his appearance?

'Then you were born nearby, perhaps?' Whisper ventured to ask.

'No, no – a long way away. I roamed wide and far in the early days. It was my idea to be part of the real world . . . .' The words were out before Bold could stop them.

'The *real* world?' she queried. 'What do you mean?'

Bold took a deep breath. 'I was born in a Nature Reserve: a place called White Deer Park.'

'A strange choice – to leave a Reserve for the world outside,' Whisper commented. 'What could be better than such protection; such a safe haven?'

'You are right, Whisper,' Bold acknowledged. 'I left my family behind – my brother and sister cubs – and other friendly creatures. I left the Park of my own free will, alone, in a spirit of adventure. I wanted to discover the things that lay outside the Reserve. But all I succeeded in doing was to become a challenge to Man and – and – suffered for my arrogance. Oh, I admit it! And now it's too late to change course. I shall never again be the strong, healthy animal my father himself was proud to have sired.'

'Alas! Poor Bold,' she murmured sympathetically. 'But tell me about your father.'

Bold grunted. 'What is there to tell about him that's not known already? It seems everyone knows his history.'

'Is he so famous then?' Whisper asked incredulously.

'Yes, he is famous – the Fox from Farthing Wood.'

Whisper drew a sharp breath. '*He* is your father? Oh, Bold . . . .' What more was there to say? The epic journey that his father had undertaken had made him a legend among the animals. Now his son had thrown that all away. *He* had only clamoured for the dangers, the excitement that his father had sought to escape.

'I can never return there,' Bold said. 'You must see that.'

'I see you have been very foolish,' Whisper said honestly, 'and yet, what a brave fox you must have been . . .' Her voice trailed off and she gazed at him with glistening eyes. It was at that very moment that an idea came into her mind that soon became a very firm resolve. Of course, Bold knew none of it. Whisper meant to keep silent until that idea should become a reality. She composed herself to sleep.

Bold stayed wakeful, despite his weariness. Their talk had re-opened old wounds, old regrets and old sorrows for him. He thought of Vixen, his mother – more graceful, more lithe, more skilful even than Whisper. Did she ever think of him? Yes, of course – she must do. But of one thing he felt quite certain. She would never see her bold, brave young cub again . . . .

—14—
Tracked

Whisper's mistaken idea of his own age made Bold determined to examine himself more closely. So, a few days
later, when the opportunity arose, he left the young vixen
sleeping in her earth, and emerged slowly and carefully
into the daylight. Nothing moved in the churchyard. The
ground was hard and rimed with frost, but the air was
clear and it was brilliantly sunny. Bold made his way to the
hole in the stone wall and slipped through; then he set his
course for the canal.

He moved along the familiar paths with extreme caution. There was no sense of bravado in this daylight jaunt.
The last jot of that had been dissipated long before. He
reached the waterside without any trouble and, with some
trepidation, peered over the bank. The water was as

smooth as silk and a perfect reflection of himself appeared, undisturbed by a single ripple. Bold gazed at it for a long moment, keeping quite still. Certainly, this image was of no youngster, but of a mature fox – an animal who had had to struggle hard to maintain a grip on its existence. The visage was long and lean. A scar over one eye ran into its corner, making it appear as if it were only half open. The fur on the head and body was not a bright red but a darker, duller hue. There was no healthy shine to be seen anywhere on the coat. The damaged leg appeared shrunken and wasted against the three healthier ones and the brush, thin and tufted, hung limply behind as if ashamed of itself. But it was the eyes of the beast that told Bold's story most vividly. There was a dullness about them and a sort of bewilderment in their expression, mixed with a sense of defeat and an overall sadness.

Bold sat down slowly and thought. What a poor specimen indeed had he become. He had been aware of the change in himself and yet, only now, did he recognize its full extent. Why did Whisper bother with a creature like him? There were other male foxes around, surely, to interest her more? Was it pity? A sort of maternal instinct? He could not be sure. Only by asking the question of Whisper herself could he understand, and it would not be easy for him to do that. For, of course, he was not sure he really wanted the answer.

He stayed no longer by that all-too-revealing stretch of water, but limped home as fast as he could. When still some distance from the earth, Bold had to take cover rather suddenly. A huge, brown dog was padding briskly in his direction with no sign of any human companion to restrain it. Bold stood amongst some almost leafless undergrowth with bated breath and a hammering heart, trusting to his camouflage. The dog came close but passed him by, seemingly bent on an errand of its own. When he was sure it was far enough on, Bold crept out and made all haste for the churchyard.

As he neared the wall two tremendous barks – terrifyingly deep and more like bellows than barks – resounded in the thin, winter air. Bold half turned, though he knew full well whence the awful noise came. The great brown dog had picked up his trail somewhere in its wanderings and was following it with an alarming rapidity. Bold stumbled to the hole in the stones and scrambled through. He did not stop to turn again. The bellows told him all he wanted to know about the closeness of his pursuer. In and out of the headstones he weaved and along the grassy ways until he was safe at the entrance to Whisper's den. Then he turned to see the dog leaping the wall and, for all its size, taking it with the ease of a gazelle.

Whisper, who was of course awake, cried out as Bold almost tumbled on top of her. 'What is it? What is it?'

'A dog,' Bold panted. 'Must have followed me. A huge brute the size of a donkey!'

Whisper cowered against him, making Bold feel twice the animal he really was. 'Don't worry,' he urged. 'It could never get in here.'

The dog could be heard moving outside. Even its hot breathing could be heard as it sniffed and slavered at the hole. Then it gave vent to a series of terrific barks, airing its frustration at the escape of its quarry. The earth reverberated to each cry.

'Oh, what can we do?' Whisper wailed. 'Why does it stay there, making those awful noises? Is there no man to call it off?'

'I saw none,' Bold answered grimly. 'But perhaps one is out looking for it now. Keep calm – it can't stay there for ever.'

The barks eventually ceased and were replaced by an

angry sort of whine. Whisper's rigid body relaxed a little. Bold ventured a comforting lick. At last the sounds abated altogether.

'Will it go now?' she whispered.

'I expect so – to vent its spleen on some other poor creature,' Bold muttered.

'Well, let's hope it won't be back,' she said. 'And, Bold, thank you – for comforting me.'

Bold glowed. Perhaps there *was* more than just sympathy in her feelings.

'Where did you go?' Whisper asked suddenly. 'You left me sleeping.'

'To tell you the truth, I went to look at myself,' he confided.

'Whatever do you mean?'

'In the canal – I wanted to see my reflection.'

'Ah. Now I understand. And I think I know why.'

'Do you, Whisper?'

'Is it because of what I said about your – er – age?'

'Yes.'

'I wish I'd said nothing. I'm so sorry to think I upset you. I just didn't realize . . . .'

'I know. But don't fret over it,' said Bold. 'It's all forgotten now.'

'I wouldn't want to do anything to hurt you,' Whisper said softly.

'Nor I you,' Bold murmured.

They fell silent, full of their own thoughts. Whisper spoke first. 'We must build you up,' she said with resolution, betraying what her thoughts had been about. 'Whatever we catch in future, you must have the greater share.'

'No, I –' he began.

'I've already decided,' she said with finality. 'You've had no start in life. At any rate, what start you did have was soon lost. You've suffered more than enough for one so young and I – I shall make it my task to help you back to health.'

'But, Whisper, I can never be really healthy again. My leg won't mend.'

'No matter. You'll have flesh on your bones, at any rate.'

Bold marvelled at her determination. 'I'm so glad I met you,' he said.

'Mine was the luck,' she countered. But she didn't reveal why and Bold was left in blissful ignorance, at least for the time being.

Whisper proved to be true to her word. Whatever they managed to find to eat, she ensured that Bold had the best of it, even if the pickings were poor. Once or twice Bold went to the privet hedge to see if Robber had been by, but there was no evidence of it.

One day in Whisper's den the pair of foxes were woken from sleep by the same dreadful bellows from the great dog who had troubled them earlier.

'He still has our scent, it seems,' Bold remarked grimly. 'We must take more care when we are out of the den.'

'Is he always going to be around then?' Whisper asked with alarm. 'I don't know what he's after.'

'Our smell has a certain effect on most dogs,' Bold said. 'A foxy odour usually makes them very excitable.' He avoided answering her question.

As before, when the dog had had enough of sniffing at the entrance to the earth, it made off. That night Bold and Whisper used a great deal more circumspection on their travels. There were no misfortunes. In fact, they struck lucky. In one garden they came across the best part of a cooked chicken tossed into a bin untasted. The rancid flavour of the meat which had been the reason for its rejection by more delicate palates, only added zest to the foxes' meal. After they had demolished the carcass and were sitting back licking their chops, Whisper said: 'You know, Bold, my idea is beginning to work. You're definitely a little plumper.'

'Am I?' he asked with surprise. 'I don't feel any different.'

'Don't you feel – just a little bit stronger?' she said. 'You do look it!'

Bold was rather flattered. 'Well, I . . .' he began. 'Yes,' he went on, 'it's not so much strength as – er – well, some of my old confidence is coming back. And that must be due to you, Whisper.'

'Perhaps I've helped,' she said. 'And if so, I'm very glad. For, after all, that was what I intended.'

And, indeed, as the days passed Bold did gain weight and stature. Even his damaged leg troubled him less. His appetite had improved, his step was less laboured but, most important, he felt differently about his future. He no longer lived from day to day. He looked forward to the end of the winter when food would be easier to find and he and Whisper (he always thought of them together now) could leave the environs of the town and return to the open country. Once again, there seemed to be some purpose in his life. In this new hopeful mood he decided to look for his friend Robber to see how he was making out.

Soon after dawn the next day Bold was on the move, first making quite certain it was safe to be so. In the pallid winter light no other living thing seemed to be wakeful. No bird sang, no small animal rustled a twig or dead leaf. Bold alone shivered in the freezing temperature. He limped around all Robber's usual haunts and finished up at the privet hedge without receiving sight or sound of him.

There he left a message in the shape of a morsel of food so that his friend the crow should know he had been around.

On the way back to Whisper's side, Bold found a stale loaf of bread thrown out for birds to peck at. Never one to miss an opportunity for some extra mouthfuls, particularly in times of scarcity, he ate the bread. Hard and indigestible, it lay heavy on his stomach and it was with a slower pace that he went towards the churchyard. He thought he heard some muffled barks in the distance but as he was close to home he thought no more of it. Mechanically Bold lurched towards the hole in the churchyard wall he and Whisper had made. For a moment he seemed to lose his direction. Then he turned and went along the wall, looking for the loose stones underneath the hole. He paused and looked around in bewilderment. There were none to be seen. A feeling of alarm gripped him. It was now well on into the morning and, while he had been on his wanderings, the wall had been hastily repaired, obviously by human hand.

As Bold stood looking at the wall with the horrible thought in his head that there was now no way in which he was capable of passing beyond it, the barks he had heard earlier were again audible, only much closer. The fox knew instinctively what creature was uttering them. In a feverish haste he continued along the wall and round the corner, vainly searching for some weakness where he might perhaps be able to force an entry. Not a chink of light showed through the stones.

The huge dog came bounding onward, eagerly sniffing at the familiar odour. Bold heard its approach and began scrabbling frantically at the wall, hoping to dislodge it. Miraculously two large stones loosened and fell inwards to the churchyard, leaving a hole through which Bold could pass his head. Now he kicked and hacked in fury with his three good legs. The hole grew fractionally in size as the seconds tripped away. But it was all too slow. With only his head and neck properly through the new hole, Bold heard the dog arrive on the scene, roaring triumphantly. He tried to back, but now the cruel, unyielding stones held him fast. With his back and hindquarters exposed to attack from the rear while he faced into the churchyard, Bold could see the den entrance only metres away. But it might just as well have been kilometres. He could not budge and any second he expected to feel the vicious fangs of his pursuer fastened at last into his helpless body.

—15—

Rollo the Mastiff

Robber the Carrion Crow had spent a lazy morning. He had enjoyed wheeling in the icy air, alighting occasionally to march in characteristic fashion over the steely ground in search of a hardy worm. He made no special effort to hunt for food as he wasn't very hungry. Carrion was plentiful in the hard weeks of winter if you knew where to look for it. It was only by chance that he visited the privet hedge. He had not thought of Bold for some days, convinced that their paths would no longer cross now that the young fox had found a mate (for Robber took this to be the case, unquestioningly). But for some reason a picture of Bold limping painfully across a field came into his mind's eye. It was then that the bird flew to the hedge bottom. Sure enough, there he found the titbit left by Bold

earlier that morning. It was only a piece of skin and bone –
hardly an edible morsel at all. But Robber knew that the
fox had not left it there as a delicacy. He must now find his
friend.

He had a rough idea of the whereabouts of the vixen's
den. He flapped into flight, coasting and flapping alter-
nately as he steered a course through the air. He heard the
dog's barks quite plainly and for some reason (he knew
not what) he associated these noises with Bold's message.
So he flew towards the noise, saw the huge beast bounding over the ground, and followed it straight to the
churchyard.

When he saw Bold's predicament, the crow's heart
sank. It seemed as if his young friend had set a trap for
himself. What could *he* do to avert disaster? The dog
could swallow *him* at a gulp. But perhaps he *could* delay
things. He dropped downwards. The dog was balancing
itself, preparing to leap the wall, and so Robber assumed
it was going to attack Bold's head. As the dog jumped,
Bold began snarling in a futile way from his stony prison.
The dog made no attempt to snap at the fox, but simply
gambolled around while it continued to bark deafeningly.
Robber flew at the massive beast, lunging with his beak in
a brave attempt to discourage it. Of course, it paid him no
more attention than if he had been a gnat.

The din, meanwhile, had awakened Whisper who at
once found her companion was missing. Fearing he was
in danger, she crept timidly to the entrance hole and
looked out, where she saw the scene being enacted.

Bold saw her emerge. 'Keep away, Whisper!' he cried
urgently. 'Go back! Go back!'

But Whisper came on. She could not stand idly by while
Bold was helpless.

'Robber, make her go back,' Bold pleaded. 'She's quite
safe in her den.'

Suddenly the dog stopped its racket and stood quite still, as Robber flew towards the vixen. In a voice as deep as a cave it said: 'What's all the fuss about? You're not afraid of me, I hope?'

Bold's mouth dropped open. He couldn't speak.

'I only want your company,' the dog went on. 'I tried to catch you before but I was too slow, and you wouldn't come out of your den. My life is very lonely. I have no companions at all. Not like you – you must have friends galore.'

Bold couldn't believe what he was hearing. It was too absurd. This huge, powerful beast – stronger than a man – had come to him in friendship. But, even then, what did he expect of him?

'I don't understand,' he muttered. 'How can I help you?' He saw that Robber had succeeded in persuading Whisper to approach no further and that the bird was, even now, preparing to launch another dive-bombing attack on the supposed enemy.

The dog began: 'Can't I just come and converse with you? It would mean –'

It broke off as Robber came sailing valiantly in and raised one massive paw to dispose of the interfering non-entity. Bold was too late to stop it. The dog gave Robber what was intended to be a warning cuff, but the blow of such a powerful beast fell like a sledge-hammer on the poor crow who immediately crumpled into a heap on the ground.

'Robber! Robber!' cried Bold agonizingly. 'Look what you've done, you brute!' he snarled at the unwitting dog. 'You've killed him!'

Whisper now came running up. The dog looked at the foxes aghast. 'I can't have done,' he moaned. 'It was only meant as a tap.'

'You don't know your own strength!' snapped Bold. 'And he was only trying to help me!'

The dog looked stupidly from one animal to the other, and then at the little black body, insensible on the hard ground. Bold thought he had the measure of this great beast who seemed to be a bit dull-witted.

'Do something useful, at any rate,' he barked. 'Get me out of this!'

While Whisper bent over the fallen bird, sniffing gently at the coal-black feathers, the dog began to batter its huge feet against the stones of the wall. In a trice the hole was large enough for Bold to free himself. He made straight for Robber. After some tense moments he looked up at Whisper gladly. 'Why, he's only stunned!' he cried. 'He's beginning to stir.'

The dog lolloped over but Bold said: 'You'd better keep back. We don't want any more accidents.'

Whisper was amused at the meek way the animal at once sat down, looking towards Bold as if waiting for the next directions from a creature only a quarter of its size. But, above all, she was proud of Bold who seemed to be entering a new phase of living up to his name.

'Is . . . is it – er – *he* all right?' the dog asked tremulously. 'I really didn't mean to do it, you know.'

'I think he will be, but he's suffered a nasty shock,' replied Bold. 'Whisper, can we do anything for him?'

'Nothing at all,' she said. 'It's just a question of time. But we might be able to aid his revival.'

'How?'

'Like this . . . .' Whisper demonstrated, breathing her warm breath over the bird.

'I see – warmth,' said Bold, and added his services. Then he turned and looked for a moment at the dog. 'You can help here, my friend, I think,' he said.

The dog was delighted and came forward eagerly, breathing out clouds of steam in the crisp air with his stentorian gasps.

Robber opened his jet-black eyes and saw the three mammals puffing and blowing together quite amicably. He tried to stand.

'Take it carefully,' Bold said. 'How do you feel?'

'Rather at a loss,' answered the bird. 'What's going on?'

'We've been mistaken,' said Bold. 'This great fellow wants to be our friend.'

'No friend of mine,' muttered Robber, ruffling his feathers. 'And I hope he has no enemies!'

'He's very contrite about it,' Bold whispered to him. 'Try to be forgiving.'

Robber struggled to his feet and tested his wings to see if their delicate bones were intact. 'I found your message and came straight away,' he explained.

Bold had to stop and think a minute. 'Oh yes,' he said. 'I see. Actually, I just wanted to see how you were making out.'

'Perfectly,' said Robber. 'At least I *was* . . . .' He directed a piercing glance at the newcomer.

'I'm Rollo,' said the dog naively. 'Rollo the mastiff.'

'Are you indeed?' Robber said grudgingly. 'Well, your master should take better care of you.'

'Yes, he should,' Rollo said warmly. 'He leaves me out in the yard in all weathers and nothing to amuse myself with. He doesn't know I get out, though. I can jump the fence!' He seemed quite proud of this announcement.

Whisper and Bold exchanged wry glances. The mastiff was obviously quite an artless sort of beast.

'Perhaps you'd better be getting back?' Bold suggested. 'Or he *will* discover you can escape?'

A look of consternation passed over the dog's great

wrinkled face. 'Oh – yes,' he said blankly. But he made no attempt to move off.

'We'll still be around,' Bold said reassuringly. 'We live here, Whisper and I. There's always another day.'

'Yes, thank you, yes,' Rollo said, greatly pleased. 'I'll certainly come again.' He started to walk away, but kept looking back at his new friends.

'Until the next time,' Whisper called.

Rollo barked joyfully and bounded away, leaping the wall elaborately as if giving them a demonstration of how he managed to jump his own fence.

'Stupid creature,' muttered Robber. 'He could have killed me.'

'But he didn't, mercifully,' said Bold. 'And we must cultivate his friendship. An animal that size could prove to be a very useful ally, one day.'

—16—
The Ties of Blood

Whisper and Bold were visited frequently by the mastiff in the ensuing weeks. Since he was only about during the day, it meant that the pair of foxes were usually roused from their sleep by one or two of his great barks, summoning them to join him. They tried to be friendly, but Rollo's visits were not always welcome, particularly if they had exhausted themselves hunting for food the previous night.

The turn of the year came and went. The winter weather had not been too cruel. Food was available – not plentiful – but, working in concert, Bold and Whisper usually found enough to eat. Towards the end of January the mating season for foxes arrived. The pair had already established a firm bond in the period they had been together and so this extension to their relationship was quite natural. Bold still wondered from time to time about Whisper's choice of mate, but dismissed his thoughts almost as soon as they took shape.

When Whisper knew she was carrying Bold's cubs she decided it was time to put the next part of her plan into operation. The winter was entering its final phase and there was no time to be lost. She and Bold were lying comfortably in their earth. Whisper said: 'Very soon we must leave here.'

Bold raised his head and looked at her quizzically in the gloom. 'Soon?' he asked. 'Before the end of winter?' He thought she was referring to their eventual return to the country.

'Certainly before the end of the winter,' Whisper answered. 'We have a long journey to make before spring arrives.'

'Journey?' Bold sounded puzzled. 'A journey to where?'

'To a safe place for our cubs to be born,' said Whisper.

'Isn't it safe here?' he asked. 'We haven't been troubled –'

'Not safe enough,' she interrupted. 'I want the cubs to be born in the Nature Reserve like you were.'

Bold caught his breath. 'White Deer Park?' he whispered.

'Of course,' she said. 'You have to take us there.'

Bold saw the sense in his mate's words but was sick at heart. For long moments he said nothing. Then he murmured, almost as if to himself: 'I never thought of returning there.'

'Not on your own – I know you didn't,' said Whisper. 'But we have to think of our offspring.'

'Yes, yes, I see the sense in it,' said Bold lamely. A

thought struck him like a flash of light. Was this the reason for her selecting him? 'Tell me, Whisper,' he said quietly, 'is this why you chose me?'

'For your knowledge of the Nature Reserve? Yes, in part,' she admitted. 'But it was your ancestry that impressed me mostly.'

Bold let his head drop on to his paws. He felt as if a heavy weight bore down on him – the weight of his father's name. 'Then it was not for myself you wished to mate with me?' he said agonizingly.

Whisper tried to reassure him. 'Of course it was for yourself,' she said. 'You have the blood of the Farthing Wood Fox in your veins. I'm proud of you. Now my cubs will make me proud too.'

She couldn't have said a more distressing thing. Bold was crushed. His mission had failed. 'Well,' he said softly, 'it seems my struggles are over.'

'Your struggles?' she echoed.

'Yes,' he said. 'Dear Whisper, had you not realized that I've been trying to forge my own destiny? All my short life I have tried to escape that long shadow cast by my father's fame. I left the Park to live life my own way – to create my own identity. Now I see I shall always live within that shadow – I can't shrug off my origins. It is my fate.'

Whisper was stunned. She couldn't speak.

'I know now,' Bold went on sardonically, 'why you preferred a crippled, haggard specimen, old before his time, to any one of a dozen, healthy young dogs. Hah! *My* only claim to fame is my genealogy!'

'Stop! Stop!' she cried. 'I can't bear any more! Why are you so bitter? You *have* created your own destiny. You've lived a braver, more resourceful life in your one year than is even contemplated by most creatures. What you did took a great deal of courage!'

'And now I go creeping back from the world I chose, with my tail between my legs!'

'You talk as if your life is over!' Whisper exclaimed hotly. 'You are to be a father in a couple of months. Your destiny now is to pass on to your cubs the knowledge and the craft gleaned from your experiences. To teach them, with me, just as your parents instructed you!'

'Yes, yes, I know the role expected of me,' Bold said wearily. 'I'll lead you to your haven of peace and tranquillity; you need have no fears.'

'We have a bright future ahead of us, Bold,' Whisper encouraged him.

Bold could not share her enthusiasm. It seemed to him as if his life consisted only of a past. Eventually he said: 'When do you want to begin?'

'As soon as you – *we*,' she hastily corrected herself, 'feel fit enough.'

The error was not lost on her mate. 'We must try and fatten ourselves up a little for the journey,' he said. 'I think I know how we might be able to do that.'

'How then?'

'Oh – don't worry. You can leave it all to me,' Bold said enigmatically. He spoke no more. Whisper assumed he wanted to sleep and settled herself down. But Bold had never felt farther from rest. So, when the sounds of Rollo's tremendous greetings echoed in the earth, he was glad of an excuse to depart.

'You needn't stir,' he told Whisper who, of course, had also been wakened. 'I'll go and see him.'

Rollo's great tail threshed the air as he saw his small friend emerge from his hole. 'It's a glorious day for scents and explorations,' he told the fox. 'I wish you'd come with me.' This was his invariable invitation.

'All right,' said Bold.

Rollo was overjoyed and spun round in a frenzy, bellowing excitedly. He was unable to believe his luck. 'Will you – will you really?' he cried.

'Yes, but I don't want to follow scents,' Bold informed him. 'Show me your den.'

'Gladly!' The dog set off at a spanking pace among the tombstones and paused by the churchyard wall. Bold went through his usual gap and Rollo landed on the other side with a thud.

'You'll have to go more slowly,' Bold remarked. 'My leg, you know.'

'I know, I know – doesn't matter,' said the delighted Rollo. 'Any pace you like.' They proceeded on their way.

'I saw your friend the crow,' said the mastiff. 'He seemed all right, for he croaked at me loudly enough.'

'Are you sure it was Robber?' Bold asked.

'Oh, yes. It was obvious he recognized me.'

'Yes. I imagine he would,' Bold said with a touch of irony, but it was lost on this simple-hearted monster.

'I want you to help me, if you will,' he said next.

'Help you? Of course I will,' Rollo boomed. 'You're my friend. What am I to do?'

'Not much really,' said Bold. 'Just feed me – and my mate.'

'Feed you? What with?'

'What do you eat?'

'Meat, biscuits – er – well, lots of meat . . . .'

'That will do,' Bold said humorously.

'You want my food?'

'No, no. Only what you don't want. Our appetites are small by comparison. But we need to build ourselves up. We're going on a journey.'

Rollo looked blank. 'Are you planning to leave here, then?' he asked.

'Yes. Whisper wants to find a safer home for the birth of our cubs,' said Bold.

'But you don't have to leave,' protested Rollo who didn't want to lose his friends as soon as he had gained them. 'Your cubs would be quite safe as long as I'm around. I'd make sure of that.'

'I'm very grateful for your interest,' Bold said carefully, 'but I hope I'd prove sufficient to the task of defending my own young ones. However, you won't be required to help, as Whisper's mind is made up.'

'I see. But how long will it take you to find the right sort of place?'

'Oh, as long as it takes us to get there. You see, she's already decided on our destination.'

'She seems to be very determined.'

'She is, I assure you.'

'I suppose, then, I won't be seeing much more of you?'

'I'm sorry to say that it does appear that way.'

Rollo's great wrinkled face wore a look of gloom. 'Could I – perhaps – come part of the way with you?' he asked with a sort of shyness that could have been absurd in such a large beast if it had not been so genuine.

'I really can't see that it would be possible, Rollo,' Bold replied gently. 'We shall be moving by night and – well, stealth will be all-important.'

The mastiff lapsed into silence until they reached his yard. It was a large open pen of bare earth surrounded by a low wire fence. There was a big wooden kennel in front of which stood an empty food bowl and another containing water. There was access to the yard from a door at the back of the adjoining house. Rollo leapt easily over the fence and went into his kennel. He re-emerged carrying two bone-shaped biscuits, which he dropped by the fence.

'That's my 'den' as you call it,' he said. 'There's no meat at the moment, I'm afraid. I ate it all.' He nudged the biscuits through a hole in the links with his muzzle. 'Try those,' he suggested.

Bold lay down and, holding a biscuit between his front paws in the same way as a dog, took a bite with his side teeth. 'Very appetising,' he pronounced after crunching it up. 'I'll take the other back for Whisper. But when will you be given meat again?'

'Tonight,' answered Rollo.

'Good,' rejoined Bold. 'Shall we come when it's dark, then?'

'Yes, do. I'll look forward to it.'

Bold turned and began his slow return to the churchyard. Although he had not mentioned it to Whisper, since the occasion when he had found the wall repaired and had tried to kick out a new hole, his damaged leg had started to hurt badly again. The pain was severe enough to make him wince at times if he brought that leg down too heavily, and so the prospect of a long journey, perhaps lasting some weeks owing to his lameness, was an ordeal he dreaded. But he was resolved that Whisper should remain ignorant.

He reached Rollo's hole in the wall and went through, still carrying the biscuit. Whisper slept so he dropped it by her and stretched himself out gratefully. At dusk the vixen awoke and found Bold by her side again. She let him sleep on while she devoured her titbit.

Bold woke eventually and told his companion about the arrangement he had made with the mastiff. Whisper congratulated him. 'A very sound idea,' she said. 'When does he expect us?'

'Tonight,' said Bold.

They left the earth together and Bold led the way back to Rollo's yard. The two foxes smelt the strong odour of fresh meat from some metres away as Rollo had nosed his meat dish painstakingly across the ground to the fence. He had refrained from tasting the food himself. So it was that Bold and Whisper heard their friend before they saw him, for the huge dog's belly, as empty as a pit, was reverberating with the most ominous rumblings.

'Rollo!' cried Bold. 'You're there?'

'I'm here,' came the solemn, deep-toned reply.

Bold now saw the meat dish close against the chain link fence. 'You haven't touched it!' he exclaimed in astonishment.

'No, I – I thought I'd wait for you,' replied the dog. 'It's more companionable to eat together.'

'Poor Rollo,' said Whisper as a fresh rumble racked the cavernous depths of his stomach. 'How you must have suffered!'

'Well, I'll do so no longer, now you're here,' he replied and took a gargantuan mouthful.

Whisper and Bold were able to hook pieces of meat through the wire with their paws, and all three made a good meal. Rollo was far too polite to take more than the two foxes did between them; neither did he tell them he could comfortably have eaten as much again. But he did ask them when they expected to leave.

'Not later than the new moon,' said Whisper.

'I shall miss you,' said the mastiff, looking at them with his great mournful eyes.

The foxes did not know how to comfort him, so said nothing on that subject. They talked for a while and then made their farewells.

'I'll be here waiting for you tomorrow night,' Rollo promised, 'with the same supplies.'

'Don't starve yourself on our account,' said Whisper kindly. 'Eat what you want first.'

'Thank you, Whisper,' said Rollo, 'but it wouldn't be with the same relish.'

'He really is a friend to us,' Whisper remarked as they left him. 'We owe him quite a lot.'

'We do,' agreed Bold, 'and it makes me sad that we have to desert him so soon.'

But Whisper's resolution was final. 'As to that,' she said, 'we have no choice. For blood is thicker than water.'

—17—

Back to the Country

The day for their departure came sooner than expected. Bold had gone at daybreak one day to have a look round for Robber to acquaint him of their intentions. He did not find the crow but he did find a message left under the privet hedge: a piece of meat still sufficiently fresh to persuade Bold that it had been dropped there that very morning while he'd been looking elsewhere. What could it mean? The crow seemed not to be in the immediate vicinity, so what was he to do? Bold decided he would go and consult Whisper.

As he approached the familiar churchyard wall, which soon would no longer encompass his and Whisper's home, he realized what Robber's message had intended to convey. The gap in the wall made by their friend the mastiff had been repaired again and so, once more, Bold had no access to his earth. Even as he looked at this new barrier there came several loud 'caws' from a nearby treetop. Bold spotted the bird among the bare branches and barked a greeting. Robber flew down.

'I think we're in need of your powerful friend again,' he said to the fox.

'No-o,' Bold said dubiously. 'Not on this occasion. The wall seals my entrance and my fate at the same time.'

'Don't talk in riddles, Bold,' Robber urged. 'What are you hinting at?'

'Oh, I've just been looking for you to tell you that Whisper and I are to embark on a journey,' Bold said casually. 'Now I can add to that piece of information. We shall start today.'

Robber was full of questions.

'It's to be White Deer Park, my own birthplace,' Bold told him. 'For the sake of my unborn cubs I'm returning to the safe haven I turned my back on only last summer.'

'Ah, so a family is in question,' said Robber. 'In that case, your young vixen is behaving very sensibly.'

'She is – I don't deny it,' Bold averred. 'Yet I can't be sanguine about my own chances of completing the journey.'

'You look more robust now than you've done for a long time,' the crow observed. 'If you take it easily . . . .'

'Yes, I've gained some weight,' Bold admitted. 'But it's an awfully long trek on only three sound legs.'

Robber re-arranged his wings and looked thoughtful. At length he said: 'I'll keep you in sight as you go. Then, if you ever should need help –'

'I'm most grateful,' said Bold promptly. 'I have to confess I was rather hoping you might say something of the sort.'

The two separated momentarily as they spotted some human figures walking close by. Robber flew back to his tree-top while Bold found cover amongst some undergrowth. When the coast was clear again the fox emerged to ask his friend to alert Whisper to their new situation. Robber flew to the earth's entrance hole and 'cawed' repeatedly until Whisper responded. She came at a run and jumped over the wall.

'Our cue to leave, it seems,' Bold said to her.

'Yes. We must hide up until dark.'

'We'll go to my old hideaway,' Bold decided. 'Robber, will you scout around and see if it's safe to proceed?'

The crow flew off at once and returned quickly. 'If you come now, you should be under cover before any fresh danger appears,' he announced.

Bold led his mate back towards the playing fields and the familiar tangle of shrubbery and undergrowth in the old waste-plot. Robber left them with a parting 'I'll look for you tomorrow'. The hours to darkness dragged by while Bold and Whisper tried vainly to sleep, their minds too aroused and full of thoughts of their undertaking. Only as the still-early dusk began to descend did they fall into an uneasy doze.

During the night they awakened to the screeches of a pair of owls calling through the trees. They looked at each other significantly.

'Time to go,' said Whisper.

'Time for one last sustaining meal?' Bold queried. He was thinking of Rollo.

Whisper knew it. 'Very well, dear Bold – if we're quick.'

Rollo's greeting was as boisterous as ever but the foxes' restraint told him the news he had been fearing. For the last time he silently pushed his meat dish across the yard. The three animals ate with glum expressions. There was no time to talk afterwards. They made hasty but warm farewells and the pair of foxes disappeared into the night. Neither cared to look back, for they both knew that poor Rollo would be standing by his fence, gazing after them with the wringingly forlorn expression he had been wearing ever since he had heard their plan.

They travelled steadily and noiselessly. Bold tried to ignore his bad leg and Whisper, of course, allowed *him* to set the pace. By dawn they had put the neighbourhood of the town behind them and were on the fringes of open country once again. A dark patch of woodland beckoned them to their rest. The murmurings of town life reached them still, but so muted as to enhance the new peacefulness of their surroundings. The night's frost, as yet undispersed, nipped at their skins and they huddled together for warmth. A delicious languor overcame them and they slumbered gratefully.

The next morning Robber followed their direction. He knew which route Bold would take. Unerringly he flew into the clump of trees that sheltered them, saw their sleeping bodies and vanished again. Now, for the bird, too, the sojourn amongst town-dwellers was over.

That night Bold and Whisper needed to hunt for food for the first time in many days. It was February and the last month of what had been a relatively mild winter. Food was still by no means abundant. The weight of their effort was necessarily undertaken by Whisper. Bold had passively to accept a lesser role and he did so almost thankfully. The difficulties of once more finding sufficient to eat meant that their travelling time was restricted. So their progress did not advance much before daylight threatened again. In this way, almost by fits and starts, the first week passed.

Bold was not displeased with their slow pace, as in that way his injured leg was not overtaxed. However, by the end of the week, Whisper was visibly fretting.

'We must make an effort to speed up a bit, Bold,' she urged. 'We've come such a little way!'

'Don't worry; there's no need,' replied Bold, who had the benefit of his knowledge of the distance to the Nature Reserve. 'We have to take time to eat.'

'It's not the eating, but the hunting, that takes the time,' she corrected him. 'If only there were some way of reducing it.'

'There isn't,' Bold said flatly. 'It was your decision to travel in the winter when food isn't plentiful.'

'I know. I know. There's no way round it, I suppose. But I can't help getting concerned.'

'Trust my knowledge – we shall do it.'

'Of course I trust you,' Whisper said tenderly. '*I* shouldn't complain when it is you who are finding it most difficult.'

The next night they were close to the farm where Bold had killed the bantam cock. There was no such rich fare for him and his mate on this occasion. They caught what small creatures they could, dug up some roots, and were glad to get them. Bold led Whisper to the hedgerow where earlier he had been dug out of his earth. He told her how he had only escaped death by a hair's-breadth of unaccountable human whim. They decided to lay up in the shrubbery during the daytime. Robber was still following them, but kept to his plan of not approaching while things went well.

Now that the pair of foxes were in an area of farmland, there were scraps and pickings to be had for a little less work. This pleased Whisper who then, naturally, tried to force the pace a little. Bold uttered no objection but simply gritted his teeth more firmly and hung on. Now, when the time came to rest, he was prostrate with exhaustion. Yet still he did not demur. As luck would have it, the weather came to his rescue.

It was the middle of February and it seemed that only now was winter about to release its worst on the countryside. The temperature had been steadily dropping and now there was a savage, new bite in the air – such as had not been felt all season through. It was as if it had been held in reserve to inflict the greater hardship when it was most unexpected. Ice formed on every small puddle, each twig was rimed with white and, at last, the snow fell in earnest. It began at night and continued around the clock. Coupled with the strong wind, it was impossible to withstand. Bold and Whisper found what protection they could amongst some holly and shuddered miserably as the wind moaned over the land. Snow was piled up against any large obstacles in drifts, and overall its mantle was spread to a depth daunting even to the largest and longest-legged of would-be travellers – Man himself.

While the wind raged and the snow fell Whisper accepted the impossibility of moving. Indeed, she tried her best to enlarge a rabbit burrow to give them more shelter, but the ground was now so hard that she could not manage to make more than a sort of depression in the soil. Here she and Bold cowered, burying their faces in their brushes, while their backs gathered snow enough to bury them. When the blizzard abated at last, Whisper was eager to press on, however tardily. Bold looked at the scene before them with more than just misgiving.

'It would be madness at present,' he declared.

'But if there's no alternative?'

'There *is* an alternative,' he argued. 'We look for better shelter and take cover until there's an improvement.'

'But think of the time we might lose,' Whisper persisted.

'Better that than losing our lives,' Bold answered grimly, '*and* those lives not yet begun.' This latter remark tipped the balance as far as Whisper was concerned and she gave in.

'Perhaps you are right, after all,' she said. 'But it mustn't be a long stay.'

Bold didn't answer. He was content to let things take their own course while they were at the dictates of the weather.

'I'll see if I can find a more promising shelter hole,' Whisper volunteered. 'We do need to go underground.' She left Bold in the hollowed-out 'form' and went deeper into the little wood. Under the trees, albeit with their bare branches, the snow was less thick than in the open. Nevertheless her search was not an easy one. At each step, her feet sank about ten centimetres and moving around, even here, was laborious. She realized Bold had been more sensible than she. A deserted hole, not quite filled and disguised by snow, lay under the half-exposed roots of an oak tree. It was just about large enough inside for the two of them and, before returning to her mate, Whisper scooped out the unwanted debris from the interior.

She and Bold were soon esconced safely inside, heartily glad to be out of reach of the worst excesses of the winter elements. The main thing on their minds now was, of course, food. But first they slept.

When they awoke it was daylight. The wind had dropped but more snow had fallen and the wood was shrouded in silence. By the entrance to their hole, which was nearly blocked up, lay a few, poor scraps. Whisper was puzzled but Bold knew at once how they came there.

'Don't you see – it's Robber!' he exclaimed. 'Even in these conditions he didn't forget us. And I bet he went short himself to spare these morsels. He'll be facing the same difficulties as any other creature.'

'How on earth did he find us?' Whisper wanted to know.

'No doubt he's had his sharp black eyes on us all along,' Bold answered with amusement. 'I'll just go a short distance and see if I can spot him.'

Bold made his way to the edge of the wood and looked out. The sun shone; the air was fresh and very cold. The landscape spread before him was a sea of brilliant white. Trees and clusters of vegetation were festooned with sparkling decoration as bright as diamonds. He was dazzled. Against that gleaming array, even the smallest bird's movements were plainly discernible. Their dark, darting little bodies stood out in startling contrast. Bold looked for a larger black shape among the snow-clad branches. He saw it. He took a few hesitant steps into the open, hoping it was indeed Robber he had spied. As if he had been waiting for a signal, the bird came winging down directly towards his friend.

'Hallo, Faithful,' said Bold good-humouredly.

'Aha! You must have found my little offering?' Robber said and uttered a croak of pleasure.

'I want to tell you not to concern yourself with us,' Bold said, 'because, my dear friend, you will have your work cut out feeding yourself.'

'It's certainly become very difficult all of a sudden,' Robber concurred. 'Just when we looked forward to the spring, too. But I *do* want to help. Now you've come this far you can't turn back and – well, finding food in *this* situation is a pretty daunting task.'

'It is,' said Bold. 'But Whisper and I have holed up in the wood here whilst we can go no further.'

'I'm going back to the town,' Robber rejoined. 'It's safer to be near humans at times like this. Then, as soon

as I strike lucky, I'll be able to bring something for you –
and more worthwhile than this time.'

'No, Robber,' Bold said flatly. 'It's too far for you to fly
to and fro for our benefit. I couldn't allow myself to be so
beholden to any creature, and I know how Whisper
would feel about it.'

'A long way by foot, yes,' agreed Robber, 'but less far as
the crow flies!'

Despite the joke Bold remained serious. 'Please, let's
say no more about it,' he said. 'Whisper and I will cope.
It's different from when I was alone – she's not handicapped in any way. And I'd be far happier knowing you
have only the worry of looking after yourself.'

'So be it,' said the bird. 'I won't press the point. At least
I know where to find you while this weather continues.
And, once it's over, I shall return to open country – for
this must be winter's last fling.'

'Good luck go with you,' said Bold.

'The same to you,' returned Robber. 'I shall be thinking
of you.' Bold made his way back to Whisper's side. They
divided the scraps of food between them and tried to
sleep again. But their appetites had only been aggravated
by the little they had eaten and sleep was next to impossible. They lay in discomfort, sometimes cat-napping,
until it grew dark.

Then Whisper said: 'I'm going to see what I can
find.'

Bold said: 'I'll come with you.'

'No,' she replied. 'I can do more on my own. I'm
sorry,' she went on, knowing Bold would feel this deeply,
'but I really think there's more chance that way.'

'You're right, of course,' he said with resignation. 'I'd
only hold you up.'

When she had gone, he pulled himself out of the hole.
He scratched around in the snow and chewed at some

stalks of grass in a desultory manner, wondering about their chances of reaching his birthplace. Whisper came back quite soon.

'We're in luck,' she said. 'Follow me.'

Bold stumbled in her wake, his spirits raised. She took him to a glade in the wood which she had discovered was rich in bluebell bulbs. She had dug up quite a quantity of them. Bold looked at the little white bulbs with a sense of irony. In these conditions, such miserable fare could assume the proportions of riches unknown. Whisper had already started eating. She looked at him with irritation.

'Don't turn your nose up at them,' she said. 'They may be all that's standing between us and starvation!'

—18—

A Lack of Patience

The halt in their progress enforced by the appalling weather proved to be a mixed blessing for Bold. His appetite, like Whisper's, was never properly satisfied, but his bad leg was rested. The lull in their activities was a good thing from that point of view. The leg had a chance to recover from the strains recently imposed upon it, and the pain seemed to subside. Five days passed with no let-up in the icy conditions. For Whisper, these were five more days lost. On the sixth day the temperature rose a few degrees. She went out of the wood to test the ground for travelling. The reverse of her expectations occurred. During the coldest temperatures the snow had frozen each night and become compacted and firm underfoot. Now it was thawing ever so slightly and, consequently, was softer and more giving so that it was more taxing to walk on. Disheartened, Whisper reported her findings to Bold.

'We must be patient,' he told her.

'I've tried to be,' she answered, 'but it's difficult for me. I've seen a previous winter, Bold. You haven't. There will only be a gradual change each day. The snow might take days to disappear.'

'We needn't wait for it to vanish altogether,' Bold said encouragingly, trying not to think of himself. 'I'm committed to this venture as well, don't forget. I'm responsible for getting you to that Reserve.'

'I'm sorry,' said Whisper softly. 'You must forgive my anxiety.'

'Of course I do,' he said. 'And I do understand, Whisper.'

The next night they resumed their journey. The ground was sticky, slippery and toilsome. After only a short distance Bold's bad leg ached and, when he paused, the three good legs trembled from the strain. He licked his lips but said nothing. Whisper also refrained from comment. On they went again. Bold's pace grew slower and slower; his limp more pronounced. The beneficial effects of their five days' rest were undone in a couple of hours. Yet he struggled on grimly, and without complaint. They came to a slight rise in the land. Even for Whisper the task of pulling herself up it when, at every step, the slush caused her to slip back, was awesome. For Bold it was torture. He could exert no pressure on his injured leg to get a grip and so he was left to flounder on three. By a supreme effort of will he reached the crest of the slope where he promptly collapsed.

Whisper looked at him in anguish. 'Oh, Bold!' she wailed. 'What have I done? We shouldn't have started – I've been so foolish!'

Bold tried to put on a brave face. 'Just need a . . . breather,' he muttered. But Whisper knew better.

'I shouldn't have forced you – oh! oh! we should have waited.'

'You didn't force me,' he replied. '*I* said not to wait longer.'

'No, no, it was my fault,' she insisted. 'My over-anxiety . . . .'

'Whisper . . . no use being wise . . . after the event,' Bold murmured. He tried to stand, staggered, and fell on his side.

Whisper was beside herself. They couldn't stay where they were, yet how could she assist him? She lay down next to him and nuzzled him; then licked at his face.

'You must take cover,' he said to her painfully. 'Before daybreak . . . .'

'I can't leave you here alone, in this exposed position,' she protested. 'Anything could happen!'

'I'll be all right. A bit longer to rest . . . then I'll follow you,' he answered.

Whisper licked at his bad leg – at the hole in his thigh left by the cruel pellets the previous autumn. It was a vain but loving gesture, and Bold appreciated it. For a while longer they lay together silently. There was no wind. The air was mild. Presently the sky began, almost imperceptibly, to lighten. Somewhere a solitary bird uttered a few sleepy, burbling notes as if it were talking to itself.

'Go!' whispered Bold.

The vixen stood up and shivered. Her coat was saturated by the melting snow. She gave herself a shake and regarded Bold anxiously. She looked around for the nearest point of cover. There was a copse poking through the greying expanse of snow on the horizon. She knew

Bold's chances of getting there were nil. 'I'll stay,' she told him. 'There's no cover.'

'I may be injured and exhausted but I'm not blind,' he answered her drily. 'You must head for that copse – for the sake of the cubs,' he added tellingly.

'But ... but ....'

'It will be light soon,' he said emphatically. 'Whisper – you *must* go.'

'I shall come back for you at dusk,' she said hopelessly. She really didn't think she would see him again – alive.

Bold said: 'I'll join you when I'm ready.' His voice sounded hollow.

Whisper went, with many a backward glance.

When the sun was fully up, Bold again hauled himself to his feet and tottered a few steps as he tried to estimate the distance to the copse. He knew he could never get across even a quarter of it. He looked around the wintry vista. Luckily, there was no sign of any large creature abroad. How long could he hope to remain un-threatened on that rather prominent knoll? It was essen-tial for him to move from there to a place of greater safety. But where?

He slipped, slithered and stumbled down the other side of the slope. His body was miserably wet and chilled through with slush and mud. The bleak February sun had no warmth in it. He was hungry, but there was no chance of his finding anything to eat. Above all, he felt lonely. How long it seemed from the days when he had revelled in his solitude. Yet it was less than one whole season! Not only had his appearance changed over those few months, but also his attitudes and desires. And most of all, now, he desired company.

There was no hope of Whisper's return until the day was over – indeed, he had insisted she stay away from him. He wondered if the thaw in the weather would induce Robber to quit the area of the town again. How glad he would be to see the crow fly up. He lay down again at the foot of the slope, utterly dispirited. He would make no attempt whatever, he decided, to start for the copse. It would be senseless in his present state. Far better to wait for Whisper.

He awoke from a troubled doze with a strong sense of another's presence. The sun was now high in the sky. He turned his head – and there stood Robber!

'I didn't want to disturb you; you looked so weary,' said the crow. 'You're quite safe – nothing else has passed this way. But why are you lying out in the open like this?'

Bold's tail had been weakly thumping up and down in his pleasure at seeing his friend. Now it stopped. 'Easy to answer that,' he said abruptly. 'I can't get any further!'

'Why, what do you mean? What's happened?' Robber demanded.

Bold explained.

'Ah, you were ill-advised to try and travel through this!' Robber remarked with his beady, black eyes fixed on the fox. 'What are a couple of days? You should have been more patient, Bold.'

'I acknowledge it, and I myself would gladly have paused longer. But I tried to do what Whisper wanted.'

'Humph! She should have thought more about you!' Robber said shortly. 'Will she be back?'

'Oh, yes, she will try to get back to me. You see, she needs me to point the way.'

'I know all about parental care,' Robber said. 'I've helped to raise several broods in my lifetime. But you should have been more cautious, the pair of you. More haste, less speed. Now you've got to pause whether you like it or not, until you can walk again.'

'It may be too late,' Bold said pessimistically. 'I don't know if I can make a recovery this time.'

'Nonsense!' Robber croaked. 'There's warmer weather coming – I know it as sure as I know that night follows day. We'll get you some food – good food – and you'll soon mend.'

Bold sighed. 'What a comfort a good friend can be,' he said thankfully. 'And, Robber, you are as good a friend as any creature could hope for.'

Robber cawed a rather more melodious couple of notes than he was wont to do. He was delighted to be held in such high esteem. Perhaps this was the magic of the Farthing Wood pledge at work on *him*, this strange willingness to help another animal in need?

'I brought this – it's not much,' he said, pushing a small dark object towards Bold with his beak.

'Carrion?' inquired the fox.

'No. Stolen goods,' answered Robber. 'What the cat didn't want.'

Bold sniffed curiously at the item. It was certainly meat, but a meat he had never seen before. However, an empty stomach needs no second bidding to be filled, and down the morsel went.

'You said something about *good* food?' Bold hinted.

'I did – and it's as good as arranged,' said the crow. 'As you can't move, I'm going to have to leave you here for a bit. I'll be back as soon as I can. In the meantime, is there any way in which you can make yourself less conspicuous?'

'Not without immediately turning the colour of my coat to white,' Bold answered sarcastically.

Robber looked at him askance. 'You've hit upon something there without intending it,' he observed. 'Why don't you dig yourself more into the snow – you'd be difficult to spot except at close quarters?'

'I could try, I suppose,' Bold said without enthusiasm. 'But I don't want to freeze to death.'

'Don't be absurd, Bold,' Robber answered. 'There's no danger in it greater than that of feeling some discomfort. Well – I'll away.'

Bold was left alone again. For some time he didn't move. Then he heard some human voices and took Robber's advice to heart. He pawed at some of the firmer snow close to the ground until he had made a makeshift sort of tunnel under the slushy surface. This at least served to hide part of his body and gave him an added feeling of security. The voices disappeared and a hush returned to the countryside. Bold lay trying to ignore his misery, by listening to the beats of his own heart and telling himself that each one brought him close to the time when Whisper might return.

A sudden noise made his heart beat much faster. It sounded again – the noise of dogs following their quarry; excitable, savage and lusting for blood. It was horrible to listen to. For any wild creature it was terrifying. And Bold could not move. Instinctively, he flattened his body. He tried to make himself as small as possible, in the nature of all animals trying to avoid detection. He could see nothing, except what was immediately in front of him. A few moments later, a hare streaked across his line of vision – running, leaping, zigzagging this way and that as it tried to shake off its pursuers. Then two long, thin dogs raced past in the little animal's wake, their pointed faces agape, and their tongues lolling between cruel, laughing fangs. Bold shuddered at their eager, frantic barks. Angry human shouts tried to call them back, but in vain. It seemed the hare should have been allowed to escape; yet now the dogs were deaf to everything but its certain

death. And the ghastly race continued. The hare doubled
back on its course, back past Bold in his fragile igloo, its
springy, elastic bounds flagging by a fraction. Desperate
to outrun each other the dogs had increased their speed,
and came on with their gleaming, murderous eyes. A
scream – thin, childlike but shattering, rent the countryside.
The hare was caught – and torn – by those ferocious
jaws.

Bold had never seen such fearsome beasts. He knew
nothing of greyhounds. Dogs that seemed to be uncon-
trolled by their human masters threatened the safety of
any animal – wild or otherwise. Despite his sufferings,
Bold simply could not bear to stay still any longer. He
crawled out from the snowy shelter, intent on one thing:
to move somewhere, somehow, away from those dreadful dogs. He started to walk blindly; mechanically. Had
he remained where he was he would have been safe. The
owners of the greyhounds had almost reached them. But
the dog who had been cheated of the kill by its faster rival
now saw the chance of another victim, as it spied Bold's
halting movements in the distance. In a trice, it ducked
the grasp of its frustrated master and launched itself on a
fresh attack.

—19—
A Friend in Need

For a bird, and a large bird at that, the distance through
the air from the point where he left Bold – back to the
town, was modest. At their necessarily slow pace, the pair
of foxes had really come no great way. So Robber was
soon among human habitations again, and now he flew
straight towards Bold's other friend.

Rollo was napping, half in and half out of his kennel,
when Robber descended and perched on the fence. He
woke at once and sprang up. 'Have you seen them? Have
you seen them?' he asked quickly.

'Yes, yes, I've seen them,' Robber replied. 'At least –
I've seen Bold. He's in a bad way. He needs food.'

'Of course he does,' Rollo said. 'Can't find it out there
in these conditions, can he?' He went at once to his food

bowl to remind himself if he had left anything from his previous meal. It was licked clean. 'Hm. I can't seem to help at the moment,' he muttered with some embarrassment, 'but tonight I –'

'Tonight's no good,' Robber interrupted peremptorily. 'How can I find him in the dark? Haven't you *anything* left at all?'

'Well, no, you see I wasn't expecting –'

'Obviously.'

'Wait a bit, though. There might be a biscuit or two ....' Rollo put his great head in his kennel to look.

'*Biscuits*? Robber echoed derogatorily. 'That's no use. He needs something nourishing. Of all the greedy . . .' he started to mutter, then thought better of it. Luckily, Rollo didn't hear.

'I've found two,' the mastiff said with great satisfaction, and carried out similar bone-shaped biscuits to those he had given his friends before.

'What he wants is *meat*,' Robber said irritably. 'And Whisper too, of course,' he added as an afterthought. 'Those won't get him moving again!'

'Moving?' asked Rollo. 'Can't he move?'

'He's exhausted himself trying to travel in thick snow,' Robber explained. 'He hasn't even any shelter.'

Rollo suddenly gave a tremendous bark. The crow nearly fell off the fence with alarm. 'What's that for?' he screeched.

'I've just remembered,' said Rollo excitedly. 'My master gave me a huge bone some time ago, but I've hardly touched it.'

'Well, where is it then?' demanded Robber.

'I buried it – you know, to save for the future.'

'Can you find it?'

'Oh, yes, nothing easier,' said Rollo. 'Now, let me see, was it over here by the kennel or – no, I think I put it near the fence.' He went over to one of the fence-posts and began to sniff. 'Of course, I could find the spot at once if all this snow hadn't covered up my signs,' he told the bird. 'But, don't worry, I'll soon have it up again.'

Robber was nearly expiring with impatience. 'Can't you be a bit quicker?' he croaked. 'We have to be back with him in the daylight.'

Rollo paused in his search and looked up. '*We?*' he asked, his deep voice tremulous with excitement. 'Am I to come too?'

'Oh, really!' cried Robber. 'How do you think a bird could carry a bone selected for a great, stupid dog like you – in its claws?'

'Of course, of course,' the mastiff answered, ignoring the insult. He renewed his efforts. Slush and mud flew in every direction as he dug furiously for the treasure, spattering Robber liberally until the bird flew to a safer spot. Robber 'cawed' angrily and began to preen himself.

At last the bone was unearthed. Rollo gripped it in his huge jaws and ran over to the crow, dropping it at his feet. 'There!' he cried. 'What do you think of that?'

Robber examined the mud-caked object with disapproval. 'I don't think anything of it,' he announced. 'You could hardly describe it as edible!'

'Of course it's edible,' Rollo answered. 'Why would I have saved it otherwise?' He started to claw the worst of the mud off. 'You see – there's a lot of meat on it,' he pointed out. 'A lovely succulent bone!' He barked once or twice – quite deafeningly – in his appreciation. Then he grasped the bone firmly once more and ran at the fence with a great leap. Dropping the bone briefly he cried: 'Come on then! What are we waiting for?'

Robber flew down and tried to pick up the two large biscuits with his beak. After juggling unsuccessfully for a while, he abandoned one and flew off with the other without a word, leaving Rollo to follow his flight.

The mastiff's powerful legs covered the ground in great bounds as he watched Robber's direction through the air. Snow, slush, mud – none of these was a barrier to his progress. He ploughed through everything like a juggernaut. The crow flew as low as he dared and found perches along the way to enable the dog to keep him in sight. So they progressed on the trail of the foxes.

The sun was dropping imperceptibly as Robber heard the first sounds of the greyhounds. As he flew on he saw the field where they had been set to course the hare. He saw the men and he saw the hare's desperate flight, and how it leapt right over the low hedge bordering the field and into open country. He saw the dogs push through the hedge after it, furious at the hare's attempt to escape, and how the men failed to stop them. Then he saw the slope where he had left Bold earlier that day and, even as he looked for signs of his friend, he witnessed the hare's inevitable demise. The men were out of the field now, trying to round up the hounds. One was taken; the other avoided capture and turned to race away. Robber saw what it was aiming for and opened his beak to screech an alarm, dropping the biscuit. He flew round in a circle, cawing frantically as he saw Rollo in the distance, still running gamely but much slower now after his long journey. The greyhound had lost none of its speed, and was closing on Bold rapidly. Robber realized that any help the mastiff might give would arrive too late. So, as on a previous occasion, he flew forward to see if he could divert the attack.

Bold had taken only a few limping steps when he heard the dog's renewed clamour. He faced about hopelessly.

But he was no hare. He gritted his teeth, preparing to fight. The greyhound's advance was now impeded by the harassing tactics of Robber. The crow had flown right into the face of the fierce hound before flapping away, causing it to veer; then immediately repeating the manoeuvre. The greyhound's greedy jaws snapped furiously but closed on air. Meanwhile Rollo approached.

At last the greyhound's supple body succeeded in getting clear of the bird and the dog impelled itself towards its target. Bold lunged at the aggressor, caught a glancing blow, staggered, and fell. The greyhound swung round and bit deep into the fox's neck-scruff. Bold yelped and tried to struggle free. But he was held fast. The fangs sank deeper into his flesh.

In the next few seconds Rollo joined the fray. The great bone he had so faithfully carried all the way was dropped and forgotten. With a mighty bellow of rage he hurled himself on the unsuspecting greyhound. The weight of his huge body drove all the breath from its lungs, so that it instantly released its grip on Bold. Then Rollo's great jaws seized it by the neck and shook it as if it had been a ferret. The hound's eyes glazed over and Rollo cast it away, leaving it for dead.

Bold lay still. Dark blood flowed from his wound and collected in his fur, dyeing it a deeper red. Rollo and Robber stood over him and watched his gasps with concern. But Bold, for once, was lucky. The greyhound's teeth had only pierced the thick fold of skin at the base of his neck by which Vixen, his mother, had carried him when a cub. No real damage had been done. He recovered sufficiently to sit up. He looked at the black crow and the huge frame of the mastiff and murmured simply: 'My friends.'

The men came up and, quite timidly, went to examine the motionless greyhound. They dared not approach

Rollo, for he was more than a match for them. His presence loomed over the entire scene. One man bent to pick up the hound, then stumbled away, cradling it in his arms. He went, whispering to its limp form as it hung laxly, more dead than alive. His companion followed him, leading the other greyhound, now a morose and much subdued animal. The sun continued to sink down into the horizon.

Bold slowly bent his head and licked carefully at some snow. It seemed to revive him a little. Robber went off to look for the biscuit.

'That really was . . . the nick of time,' said Bold, referring to the mastiff's entry into the mêlée. 'But wait – I don't know yet why you're here, all the way from home.'

'Wait, and I'll show you,' boomed Rollo. He retrieved the bone and came back, swishing his tail. 'There wasn't any meat left, you see,' he explained, 'when your friend the crow came for food. It's the best I could do.'

Bold sniffed at it elaborately. 'It has a very rewarding smell,' he said with amusement, 'but it looks as if it's been underground for years.'

'Oh, no – not years,' Rollo corrected him innocently. 'I think I buried it last week some time.'

'I see. Well, it shall be eaten,' said Bold. 'But I'll wait until Whisper can share it.'

Now Robber came with the biscuit. 'Eat that, at any rate,' he said. 'You've got to eat, Bold.'

'Of course,' said Bold, and he ate the stale biscuit with great relish.

As the sun sank further Robber went to roost. Rollo remained where he was. Fox and dog watched the sky darken and waited for the return of Whisper. It had been night for two hours before they saw her figure approaching through the gloom. Her relief at finding Bold almost exactly where she had left him soon changed to alarm at his wounds. But he made light of them.

'I'm lucky to be alive, Whisper,' he said, and Rollo had the great pleasure of hearing himself named as Bold's deliverer. The mastiff could not contain his delight and gambolled around the re-united foxes like a puppy.

Whisper set about licking Bold's hurts. Her touch was soothing. Afterwards they lay down, just where they were, to tackle Rollo's bone. The mastiff himself was forgotten now that they were together again.

Rollo wandered a little way off, unmindful of their neglect. He was happy just to be near them and he felt he never would forget this wonderful time when he had been at hand to rescue his friend. He sprawled on the melting snow at a distance, still near enough to offer his protection if necessary. He had no thought of returning home until, at least, the sun rose again.

After the fretful events of the day, the night was peaceful and untroubled. Bold and Whisper were kept busy by the bone for an hour or so; but they realized they would have to move before it got light. After his long rest, Bold felt ready to test his leg again. He and Whisper shook themselves free of the worst of the wet snow and called to Rollo. He came up at once.

'We have to find somewhere to hide up in the daylight,' Bold explained. 'I can never thank you enough for what you did . . . .'

'I'll stay with you as you go,' Rollo offered. 'Then, if you need any help I'll still be around.'

'But what of your master?' Whisper inquired. 'Won't he be missing you?'

'No, no . . . it's not likely,' Rollo answered, rather sorrowfully. 'I'll return when it's daylight.'

So the three animals set off again through the slush and mire. Bold's bad leg had stiffened up again and he winced visibly for the first few metres. After that it loosened a bit, and they were able to proceed a little less slowly. The remaining snow was melting fast, revealing great patches of grass. Pools of water collected everywhere and new rivulets ran over the ground wherever it was not quite flat. Water seemed to seep into everything and soon the coats of the three beasts were soaked and matted with mud. But the night was mild and windless so that their discomfort was not extreme.

'We must try and find some piece of cover nearer than that copse,' Bold panted, 'and, in any case, we don't want that direction.'

'There doesn't appear to be much available except dead bracken,' Whisper remarked.

'Well, if that's all there is – it'll have to do,' Bold answered. 'We should at least be well camouflaged if we can find a thick clump. I really can't go very far, I'm afraid.'

'Of course,' Whisper reassured him. 'We must think of you now, first and foremost.'

They discovered a patch of soggy dead bracken, beaten almost flat on the ground. But it was just thick enough for them to crawl underneath and conceal themselves.

'Where's Rollo?' Bold asked suddenly.

'He's probably started on his homeward journey now we're settled,' answered his mate.

However, shortly afterwards, up came the faithful dog again, carrying something in his jaws. It was the remains of the dead hare. 'Why waste it?' he asked, after depositing it by his friends. 'There's a good meal for each of you in that carcass.'

'There certainly is,' agreed Whisper. 'Why ever didn't we think of it?'

As dawn approached Rollo sadly bade his friends farewell, and they watched his huge lumbering form trotting, with many a backward glance, in the direction of home. The mastiff retrieved his bone on the way, for most of it was still left and it was not in his nature to abandon such a choice morsel.

When he was close to his home yard it was broad daylight, and he received the surprise of his life. His master, who had noticed his absence, was combing the area for his huge pet in great concern. When he saw Rollo coming towards him he was so relieved he ran up to the dog and made such a fuss of him as he had never done before. The enraptured dog dropped his bone and danced around, covering his laughing master with mud and uttering the most vociferous bellows in his joy. Then Rollo leapt his fence, still barking, while his master prepared to give him a thorough scrub. Now it was the foxes' turn to be forgotten as man and dog renewed their friendship in a way that made them both realize that they could never ever lose it again.

—20—
The Parting

Each night thereafter Bold and Whisper continued their journey. When the last of the snow had disappeared, food became more readily available. Now that the approach of spring was heralded, more small creatures were on the move. Whisper no longer made any attempt to force the pace. She knew that she and her unborn cubs depended on Bold entirely. She was more solicitous than ever for his well-being and did not comment on the fact that his pace was becoming slower and slower. Of course, Bold himself was well aware of it. Every night he wondered if his leg could endure yet more strain on the morrow; yet somehow he managed to keep on. Robber still followed their stages by day and he, too, noticed how the distances they covered were becoming progressively shorter.

Gradually and very, very gradually, the foxes' destination grew closer as the month of March was ushered in. They passed the ditch where Bold had first hidden after his injury. He showed Whisper the actual place where he had been shot and she looked very solemn. Then he told her of the game coverts nearby that really had been the cause of all his trouble and he mentioned Shadow the sow badger.

'You've certainly not lacked for friends,' Whisper remarked.

'No. I *have* been lucky.' Bold thought for a moment. 'You know,' he said, 'I'm obliged to admit that I wouldn't be here now if I hadn't had their help. Each time I've been in dire trouble one creature or another has come to my rescue. First of all there was Shadow; then Robber saved me from starving. Then, dear Whisper, you yourself came on the scene; and finally, poor simple Rollo. I could have died several times over without you all . . . .'

'But you yourself haven't been slow to do good turns,' Whisper reminded him. 'And anyway, Bold, it wasn't your fate to die too soon.'

'Fate?' he muttered. 'And what *is* to be my fate?'

'To lead me to White Deer Park and to see your young ones born and brought up there.'

'I suppose so,' he replied, thinking how different it was from the destiny he had planned for himself. By a strange coincidence Bold at that juncture happened to be passing a puddle of dark water where the moon and stars were reflected like a handful of diamonds and pearl. He stopped and looked at his own peering face. Shadow would have been a fitter name for *him*, for shadow he was of his former self. He saw himself as an animal dying of a lingering disease, for which there never was, and never could be, a cure. He actually shivered at the sight of his own image and hastily passed on. He said nothing; neither did Whisper – but the moment was charged with their own recognition of its significance. Bold knew then – finally and incontrovertibly – that he would never enter White Deer Park again. If he didn't die in the attempt of leading the vixen to its borders, he would absent himself from her company when she was close enough to need him no more. For his re-appearance in the Nature Reserve would be, for him, an admission of failure. Only by living alone for as long as his blighted life might last could he retain his self-respect. And that was all that remained to him. He had not been independent; neither had he enjoyed total freedom. He had only survived to this point because others had succoured him when in need. But he would regain his independence at last. He could at least die alone.

Bold gave no utterance to his thoughts and Whisper was left to think her own. Something of his feelings communicated themselves to her but she dared not voice her fears. And so they continued.

They went close by the game wood but, this time, Bold had no intention of entering it. He did not care to renew his acquaintance with the female badger, neither did he wish to court the dangers of traps and gibbets. At length he and Whisper reached the open downland. Will-power alone had enabled Bold to keep going through pain, weakness and exhaustion. Now he knew that a few more stages would take them near enough to the Reserve for Whisper to manage alone. That night, after the vixen had caught their frugal supper, she started to question Bold again about their destination.

'It won't be long now,' he promised her. 'Patience and

caution have brought us this far and should see us through.'

Whisper looked at him penetratingly. 'Can *you* keep going?' she asked. 'I've been worrying and worrying about you.'

'Worry no more,' Bold said. 'I'll last the course.'

His cryptic remarks did not reassure her. She tried to probe his thoughts. 'Once we're in the Park you need do nothing but rest and eat. I'll find us a den – or I'll dig one myself.'

Bold remained silent.

'Will we see the Farthing Wood – er – your father?' she asked. 'And your brother and sister cubs?'

'If they're still alive,' he answered evasively. He thought of Vixen, his mother, with regret. How he longed to see her once more. But it couldn't be.

Whisper fell silent, but she continued to wonder about Bold's intentions. Five more days and nights passed. Then she wondered no more. She woke from an uneasy sleep amongst some budding undergrowth to find Bold gone. She jumped up and went carefully into the open. Although she scanned the landscape in every direction, there was no sign of him. The event she had dreaded had occurred. She searched the nearby wood, calling to him in the vixen's characteristic way. Then she started to explore further afield. Copses, undergrowth and even dead vegetation she searched, always looking for an earth where he might have hidden himself. She found nothing. Then she wondered if Bold might have returned to the spot where they had last been together, while she had been looking for him in vain. She went back to their hideaway.

When she again found no trace of him she lay down miserably. She decided to wait, for perhaps he would return at nightfall. Dusk fell and her hopes were raised. But the night wore slowly on and she remained quite alone. She ate nothing. She wanted nothing – except Bold's return. She slept.

In the daylight she knew he would not come back. But still she stayed. Then, when darkness came again she knew she had to move on. Her time was approaching and now her duty to her unborn cubs was paramount. She made herself eat for their sakes and, continuing resolutely in the direction she and Bold had travelled all along, she approached the Park. As she went she still looked for signs of her lost mate wherever she thought there was any chance of finding him. But she soon realized it was a hopeless task, for by now it was obvious to her that Bold had parted from her for good. Two nights later she stood before the boundary fence of White Deer Park. Safety and protection beckoned her inside, yet she hesitated. Added to the sadness and emptiness she had been experiencing for the past few days there was now a feeling of remorse as she thought of the choice she had forced poor Bold to make. He had succumbed to her entreaties for a safe home for their cubs, whilst all along he had had no wish to return to his birthplace. He had sacrificed his own chances of survival by ensuring that his mate should reach her destination. His struggles on the long journey had been only too apparent to her, and she had seen him grow weaker with each day. Now she had lost him – for Whisper knew in her heart that Bold had gone away to die.

She stood forlornly on the threshold of *her* new world with the most bitter regrets gnawing at her conscience. Yet she felt that Bold had accepted her wishes because he himself wanted his cubs to be born in safety, even if he had decided it would mean his own life was over. She found the selfsame gap in the fence from which Bold had left his old home, and entered the Park. Giving herself a shake, she set her mind to the task of finding an earth. There was not much of the night left.

As dawn crept over the Reserve Whisper took cover. She had encountered none of the inhabitants of her new home as yet, and now she automatically took her usual precautions. She was very tired and was glad to rest. During the day she woke briefly to see a herd of white hinds stepping daintily through the grass. She had never seen such large animals before but she knew there was nothing to fear from them. Bold had long ago described all the animals she might meet at her journey's end.

In the evening she resumed her explorations. A wooded part of the Park attracted her. Under an ash tree a small animal had built a hole. Whisper began to excavate with the intention of enlarging it into a den. As she halted once from her work, she found another fox watching her. It soon became apparent that the animal was another vixen; very young; and in the same condition as herself.

'I'm sure I've never seen you in this wood before,' said the vixen, in a not unfriendly way.

'No – nor in the Park,' Whisper added.

'Oh? You've come from the outside?' Her astonishment was obvious.

'Yes, from outside. You see – I'm soon to have a litter of cubs and I wanted protection for them.'

'Indeed! May I ask how you know of the Nature Reserve?'

'Why not?' Whisper decided to cast caution to the winds. 'Their father was born here.'

The vixen gasped. '*Born* here ... but ... but ...' she stammered, 'where is he now? Oh, tell me where he is!'

Whisper realized she might have encountered one of

Bold's relatives. 'I don't know,' she wailed. 'He parted from me whilst I slept. I don't know where he is now, but – oh! he's outside the Park somewhere. He didn't want to come back here ... in spite of his mate ... and his unborn cubs,' Whisper ended miserably.

'Describe him to me, do!' begged the other vixen. 'It's very important.'

Whisper bowed her head. 'I'm afraid that would serve no purpose,' she said with a sad expression. 'You wouldn't recognize the description. But I know he was known here as Bold.'

'Bold!' cried the vixen joyfully. 'I knew it! My brother cub!'

'Your brother? Then you must be –'

'Charmer,' interrupted the vixen. 'But tell me everything, please, everything! Oh, we must find him and bring him here. Our father and mother – and my own brother – all live here still. He must come back, he must!'

Whisper felt more downhearted than ever. How could she tell Charmer that her brother might be close to death? Before she could say anything, Charmer was asking her name.

'Bold gave me the name of Whisper,' she answered almost inaudibly, so great was her emotion, 'because of my stealth.'

Charmer's eyes shone. 'Our cubs shall be cousins, Whisper,' she said excitedly. 'They will grow up together.'

'Do you have an earth in this wood?' Whisper asked.

'Yes, just a few metres from here. Shall I help you prepare yours?'

Whisper declined her offer. 'You're very kind,' she

said, 'but I prefer to manage things myself as far as my family goes.'

'I understand,' said Charmer. 'You're quite right – and I'll leave you. Do I have your permission to inform my parents of your arrival here?'

'By all means,' Whisper answered sweetly. 'They and I – and you, too – have a mutual bond. They have a right to know.'

'I will come and see you again, Whisper, to hear your story,' said Bold's sister vixen. 'I hope we might be friends. My brother chose his mate well.'

—21—
The Farthing Wood Fox

Bold's last look at Whisper was one of tenderness as she lay dreaming. Her limbs twitched occasionally and from time to time a flicker passed over her face as she followed her imaginary adventures. Bold watched. He was glad he had been able to bring her thus far, though at such cost to himself. Now she would have no difficulty in completing her journey. He stood up shakily and looked out on the sunlit countryside. Spring was approaching. In but a few weeks he would have been one year old.

Bold knew he would not live that long now. But *his* cubs would be born and the whole cycle would begin anew. Now he must make himself scarce. He had not long to reach his hiding-place before Whisper might come looking. With one last affectionate glance at his mate, he hobbled away.

From a high, high branch of a poplar tree, Robber the Carrion Crow watched Bold turn his back on the vixen. He watched in earnest as Bold limped slowly over the wet ground. Where was he going? He decided to investigate. Maintaining a discreet distance to the rear of the fox, he flitted from one tree to another, always keeping him in view. Bold went towards a spinney of silver birch through which he and Whisper had passed the previous night. To and fro he went through the dappled tree-trunks. Robber surmised he was looking for something. He flew closer. Bold had found a hollow log – all that remained of an ancient beech tree. It lay on its side, encrusted with lichen, moss and fungi. As Robber flew up, the fox bent and slunk inside. Robber perched on top and waited. Bold did not re-appear. The bird assumed he had found something to eat inside – or that he was sleeping. He fluttered to the ground and strutted to the open end of the log. He could then see his friend quite clearly. Bold was lying with his head on his paws, but was still quite awake.

'Robber!' he exclaimed. 'Wherever did you spring from?'

'I didn't "spring" from anywhere,' the crow answered. 'I flew here – as usual. Bold, what are you doing?'

'That's my affair,' came the reply.

'Of course – if that's how you feel about it,' said Robber haughtily, and made as if to go.

'No – stay. Robber, stay,' Bold said hastily. 'I'm sorry. Why shouldn't you know?' He paused.

'Well?'

'I'm going no further,' said Bold slowly. 'Whisper must finish the journey by herself.'

'But why, when you've come so far?' asked Robber.

'Look at me,' said Bold, 'and look hard. How much do I resemble even the beast *you* once knew?'

Robber shifted his feet awkwardly. 'But I'm sure, once you reach the Reserve again you'll soon –' he began.

'I'll soon be dead,' Bold cut in harshly. 'Let's be realistic. I've brought my death closer forcing myself on and on, night after night. I've done what I promised –I've shown Whisper the way. Now her cubs – *our* cubs –will be safe. But I won't ever see them.'

'That is a very sad remark,' Robber said.

'It's true nonetheless. Even if I should continue from here, I should never survive long enough for that.'

Robber looked away uncomfortably. 'She'll come searching for you,' he said.

'I know she will. But she won't find me,' Bold answered. 'I'm going to block up this entrance.'

'How ever can you do that?'

'Oh, there's plenty of dead leaves and grass and such like I can rake together.'

'I don't like the thought of it,' said Robber. 'You might perish in there.'

'You know, Robber, by all the laws of Nature I should have perished already,' replied the fox fatalistically. 'Do you remember my boast of living the True Wild Life? Well, I haven't. My life has been as protected outside the Reserve as it would have been inside – only in a different way.'

'Not true,' Robber disputed. 'You wouldn't have been *shot* in a Nature Reserve.'

'Foxes have been shot – even there – by poachers,' Bold informed him. 'But what's the point of arguing? You've been a good friend to me.' He got up and stumbled to the end of the log. 'I've no time to lose,' he said, beginning to scrape together the leaf litter where

Robber stood, into a pile.

Robber noticed that Bold found even this a difficult task, although he was using his front paws. He was swaying from side to side in his weak state. The crow tried to be helpful by picking up leaves and grass in his beak and dropping them on the mound.

'Please don't trouble,' said Bold. 'I'll get it done, even if it is the last thing I ever accomplish. You should go now, Robber, before you give the game away.'

'Very well,' said Robber. 'But I shan't stray far. I fear for you.' He left the poor struggling fox reluctantly, convinced now that the end was near.

Later in the day he saw Whisper set off on her sad, fruitless search. Bold's precautions proved to be unnecessary as she did not go anywhere near the spinney of silver birch. The next day Robber saw the vixen waiting for him still. He yearned to fly to her, to greet her with the news of Bold's lair. Yet he baulked at such an act of betrayal.

The next day Whisper was gone. Robber knew she must have reached her objective. He waited no longer. Finding what food he could, he swooped down to the beech log. 'Bold! Bold!' he croaked. 'It is I – Robber!' He heard nothing. He 'cawed' loudly four times and then began feverishly to peck at the bundle that sealed the log's entrance. He cleared a space and peered in, his head on one side. Bold was there, lying quite still.

'Bold?'

'Yes, I'm ... still here,' came the animal's weak voice.

'Thank goodness! cried Robber, who had suffered a fright. He went back for the food and brought it inside.

Bold slowly raised himself. 'Can't ... eat that,' he muttered. 'No point now.'

'Yes, yes, there is,' beseeched the crow. 'Whisper has gone, but you can still live. You *must*.'

'No . . . appetite,' said Bold.

'Try. You'll feel better. Try!'

Bold licked at Robber's offering, then took it in his mouth obediently. Robber watched him with gratification.

'I'll fetch more,' he promised, and wasted no time in setting about it.

When he returned, Bold had quitted his hollow trunk and was stretched on the grass, blinking in the March sunlight. Robber pushed a dead fledgling towards him, still almost bald, that had dropped from its nest. Bold grunted. 'You crows have . . . catholic tastes,' he managed to say.

'Bold, it's not too late to change your mind,' Robber said urgently. 'I've seen the Park. It's not far away.'

'I know you mean well,' said Bold. 'But you are wasting . . . your breath. My mind . . . is made up. I can't hunt – I can barely walk – would you have me remain alive and pampered with food while I lie almost helpless, like a Queen Bee?'

'You make your point well,' said Robber. 'What do you intend to do then?'

'I shall stay here,' Bold answered. 'The log will be my home until –' He left the rest unsaid.

The fledgling still lay where Robber had left it. 'Won't you eat this?' he asked.

'No.'

'What shall I find for you then?'

'Find me nothing and I shall be content,' said Bold enigmatically. 'And why do you stay with me? You should be looking for a mate.'

'I shall do so,' answered Robber. 'Eventually.'

Bold knew what he was thinking. 'You haven't long to

wait, my faithful friend,' he told him.

The Farthing Wood Fox and his Vixen had remained together even when their cubs had grown and departed. Their inseparability made their relationship a unique one indeed among foxes. So when Charmer visited their earth with her startling news, they heard it together. In the darkness their faces were inscrutable, but their voices betrayed their emotion.

'I always believed he was still alive,' said Fox huskily. 'Bold had the mark of a survivor.'

'But why doesn't he wish to return here?' Vixen asked. 'Why has he left his mate before his cubs are even born?'

'Whisper didn't tell me that,' said Charmer, 'so you must ask her yourself.'

'There's no need to ask,' said Fox. 'Bold is a proud animal. To return to White Deer Park would mean a loss of face.'

'You are right, Fox,' said Vixen. 'I know you are – and yet I also know it to be an absurd notion. Pride can be stretched too far. How can loss of face be important when all his family long to see him?'

'Those closest to him would be the very ones to fuel his sense of failure,' said Fox who understood such things. 'And so it's necessary for us to go to him as he won't come to us.'

'How can we? Even Whisper doesn't know where he is,' said Charmer.

'If Bold led his mate to the Reserve he is still close at hand,' Fox remarked. 'And we shall find him. *We* must all go – and Friendly his brother too – to look. But first, we should make the acquaintance of the new young vixen in our midst.'

Whisper was a little abashed to see Charmer leading

the famed Fox and Vixen – as well as a strange young male fox – towards her. But their unfeigned delight in seeing her soon put her at her ease. When they explained their plan she looked at their eager faces compassionately.

'I don't know how you will find him,' she said. 'But, even if you do, you must be prepared for the worst. Even now it may be too late.'

'Too late? Why, how can it –' Vixen began.

'Bold is not the animal you once knew. He is older and wiser for his adventures, but he has suffered a great deal. His energy and physique are severely depleted. He received a terrible injury, long before he and I encountered each other, and he has never recovered from it. The journey he undertook at my behest to bring me to safety was – I freely admit it – too great an ordeal. During the last few days we were together he was failing visibly . . . .'

'Are you telling us, Whisper,' Vixen asked, barely audibly, 'that Bold is . . . dying?' The last word came out as a long sigh.

Whisper groaned. 'Yes,' she whined, 'I believe that to be so.'

'Then we must go at once!' cried Friendly. 'Father, Mother, we must leave now!'

'Can he be so close and yet . . . so far . . . from us?' Vixen whispered.

'We can save him, surely?' Friendly asked hopelessly. 'We're not too late?'

'I fear . . . the worst,' Whisper muttered.

Bold's family looked stunned. To have received such unexpected good news and then for their hopes to be dashed almost at the same moment was awful. Vixen made the first move to go.

'Whisper – you will come with us?' Charmer asked.

Whisper looked away, into the distance, as if she were picturing Bold as he now might be. She drew a deep breath. 'No,' she answered at last, in a low voice. 'I don't think I could bear it.'

Charmer hung her head, sensing, but not wishing to see, her anguish.

'We must trust that we can bring you good news,' Fox said, much moved.

Vixen led her family away in the direction of the Park's boundary fence. Whisper stood to watch them, unmoving. Then, with a toss of her head, she turned to finish preparing her earth.

Outside the Reserve the four animals divided, the two foxes taking one course; the two vixens, another. It was a black, cloud-covered night and, for the two young beasts, Friendly and Charmer, quite an adventure. Neither of them had ever been beyond the Park's bounds, and each kept close to its parent. Fox and Vixen knew the terrain from of old and began systematically to comb the area. The hours of darkness passed with no clue found.

Charmer watched the grey dawn break with misgiving. 'Should we remain here to be seen?' she asked her mother nervously. 'Wouldn't it be better to return home until the next night?'

Vixen nuzzled her gently. 'I understand your fear,' she answered. 'But there will be no danger if we are careful. We can't afford to lose many hours in idleness.'

Friendly was experiencing the same qualms but preferred not to let his father know.

The early morning light took on a pearly quality as the birds began to sing in greater and greater numbers. One solitary bird saw Vixen and Charmer and wondered at their activity. As he wheeled on the wing in search of his breakfast he saw the other two foxes behaving in the same busy manner. Ignoring his empty stomach, Robber alighted on a branch and pondered. The more he pondered, the more he became convinced that he knew who the animals must be and what they were doing. He croaked to himself, wondering if he should become involved. He was not sure of Bold's wishes. And yet, and yet . . . if one of these animals was the Farthing Wood Fox, he, and he alone of all the creatures around, had the chance of reuniting father and son. He hopped up and down the branch in his anxiety. If he did nothing, they might never meet again – or, worse still, the meeting might be too late . . . . He simply *couldn't* allow such a sad event to happen when he might be the one means of preventing it. He 'cawed' twice to steel himself and flew down towards Fox and Friendly.

The animals looked up but paid him no attention. A crow was a commonplace enough sight, even in the Reserve.

Robber croaked nervously. 'Er – er – are you searching for someone?' he asked with awkwardness.

Fox looked at the bird in surprise. For a moment he said nothing. Then, ever cautious, he answered: 'Who are you, that you ask such a question?'

'A friend, I hope,' Robber muttered, still very much in awe of the Fox. 'I think I may be able to help you.'

'Do you have a message for us?' asked Friendly.

'No. But I must identify myself,' Robber pulled himself together. 'I am called Robber by my friend the fox – the one whom I think you must be seeking?'

'Ah!' Fox and Friendly exchanged glances.

'You are the Farthing Wood Fox?' Robber asked the senior animal.

'Yes.'

'Then I *can* help you. I can take you to Bold.'

'Do so,' Fox answered at once. 'We shall learn your history later.'

Robber signified the direction. 'You must run fast,' he said. 'I'll point out the way. You've still quite a distance to cover.' He took to the air. The two foxes ran underneath his flight path. Robber led them to where Vixen and Charmer were located and kept flying on, leaving the explanations to the foxes. He dipped and turned once to make sure they were following. The four animals were running as hard as they could. Robber kept on to the birch spinney.

Only a metre or two away from the great log, Bold lay amongst the sprouting grass and the remains of the winter's dead leaves. He was in no pain now. He felt calm. He had no desires. He was now too weak to move and he knew he would die where he lay. He saw Robber alight close by on a birch sapling and was glad. Despite his decision, he was glad he would not die entirely alone. He closed his eyes gratefully.

When he next opened them he saw, as through a mist, four familiar and beloved shapes and faces. He blinked slowly, thinking he was a cub again back in White Deer Park. Vixen came forward, sniffed, and nuzzled him with a very real tenderness. Bold blinked again.

'You're alone no longer,' Vixen whispered, 'my brave, bold cub. We will stay with you.'

A feeling of peace – almost of happiness – engulfed the stricken animal. He saw his father and his brother and sister cubs. 'Is Whisper. . . .' Bold tried hard to speak.

'Whisper is well,' Vixen said soothingly. 'Rest now. She will soon be a mother and we shall keep watch for her and bring food for her when necessary.'

Now Fox came closer. 'Your cubs will be fine, sturdy youngsters, Bold, with you for a father. My, what a stout, plucky cub you were!' Then he lowered his voice so that only Bold could hear his words. Not even Vixen overheard. 'You are a courageous animal,' he said, 'and your adventures will be remembered as long as mine. *I'm* proud to be *your* father.'

A sigh escaped Bold's parted lips. He felt a sense of release. All had not been in vain. He looked joyfully towards the black, watchful figure in the birch tree, and prepared to leave, at last, the real world.

Epilogue

In the spring Whisper's cubs were born. There were four of them – two male and two female. Charmer produced her litter, too, and so the blood of the Farthing Wood Fox renewed itself in the third generation. But Whisper had another reason to be proud, for in her cub's veins was mingled also the blood of Bold, her chosen mate. Only now could her regret at losing him be effaced by seeing his image reproduced in her offspring. As her cubs would mature and grow up, it would be Bold's history they would hear as they nestled around her in their earth. They would remember the father they would never know as the heroic creature she believed him to be, who had sacrificed himself for their well-being.

Robber came to tell her he had found a mate and, before he bade her farewell, they reminisced a little. They talked of Bold, and of their adventures, and remembered Rollo. They parted with affection.

And Whisper was never to feel lonely. Apart from Bold's family, there were new friends to be made all the time – Bold's friends and his father's friends from their old home. She soon learned that life in White Deer Park was quite unlike her previous existence.

Two months passed; her cubs gambolled in the sun and grew bigger and stronger and learnt how to hunt. One night Whisper's special friend – Charmer – came to talk. They lay on the ground by Whisper's bolt-hole, watching Tawny Owl swooping silently through the summer evening.

'My cubs wanted to know what's outside the Park,' Whisper remarked. 'I tried to explain but couldn't find the right words. I have to find a way of justifying their father's actions without persuading them to copy him.'

'This Park can be a paradise,' Charmer said. 'That's what they should learn.'

'*I've* learnt it,' Whisper answered. 'There are creatures here on the best of terms who would be tearing each other to pieces anywhere else.'

'It's a friendship that's rooted in the old Oath and worth preserving,' Charmer said.

'And a means of persuasion, perhaps, for any animal who might develop itchy feet,' Whisper added.

'I think you and I between us, Whisper, can find a more telling cure for that problem,' said Charmer humorously. 'When our cubs are a little bigger they must be encouraged to mingle. And the rest can be left to Mother Nature!'

IN THE GRIP OF WINTER

Colin Dann

The sequel to the award-winning 'The Animals of Farthing Wood'.

Fox, Kestrel, Badger, Toad, Mole, Adder and a host of other small animals have all helped each other on the perilous journey from their threatened home in Farthing Wood to what they believe to be the safety of the White Deer Nature Reserve. But the animals soon discover that their troubles have only begun. . .

Faced with one of the hardest winters on record and hunted by poachers who have stolen into the reserve, the animals of Farthing Wood must band together once again if they hope to survive.

BLACK BEAUTY'S FAMILY 1

Diana and Christine Pullein-Thompson

Here are two stories about Black Beauty's relations. Black Romany, three generations before Black Beauty, was a well-bred horse who lived at Belvoir Castle. He hunted with Prince Albert and had lots of exciting adventures trekking across England. Blossom, six generations later, was not so lucky. The product of an unfortunate alliance, she had a life of drudgery working as a cart-horse, and her future seemed bleak until, out of the blue, came unexpected success.

STRANGERS IN THE HOUSE

Joan Lingard

Calum resents his mother remarrying. He doesn't want to move to a flat in Edinburgh with a new father and a thirteen-year-old step-sister. Stella, too, dreads the new marriage. Used to living alone with her father, she loathes the idea of sharing their small flat with Willa, the silent Calum and his irrepressible young sister, Betsy. Stella's and Calum's struggles to adapt to a new life while trying to cope with all the problems of growing up are related with great insight and poignancy, in a book which will be enjoyed by all older readers.

THE CALL OF THE WILD

Jack London

Buck is a dog who has been born and raised on a rich estate in California and is used to a life of ease and security. But one day he is stolen and sold as a sledge dog. This is the story of how he adapts to life in the frozen north and becomes famous.

Jack London's gripping book has now become a classic and is not to be missed by readers of ten and over.

THE MILL HOUSE CAT

Marjorie-Ann Watts

Gladys didn't expect an answer when she asked the cat his name, but that was just the first of the surprises Oswald had in store for her and the beginning of their adventures together.

THE MILL HOUSE CAT is the enchanting story of a cat with mysterious powers.

WILD JACK

John Christopher

Privileged people are protected in walled cities from the Outlands, where Savages and wild beasts live. Clive, pampered son of a wealthy Councillor, is taken prisoner by Wild Jack, the notorious Savage – and, surprisingly, has to make the most dramatic decision of his life. . . .

Set in a future world stricken by the energy crisis, this is a topical and exciting story for older readers.

AGATON SAX AND THE CRIMINAL DOUBLES

Nils-Olof Franzén

The small town of Bykoping in Sweden is famous for only one thing – it is the home of Agaton Sax. Being a world-famous master detective makes him a target for the criminal underworld, and two dastardly gangleaders, Octopus Scott and Julius Mosca, fly in to deal with him. But their arrival coincides with that of the unfortunate Charlie MacSnuff and Absalom Nick, who keep being arrested as they are the doubles of Scott and Mosca. The ensuing muddle defeats everyone – or almost everyone!

A wonderful blend of humour and excitement for readers of eight and over.

THE WINTER VISITOR

Joan Lingard

Who is the stranger who turns up one day in the little Scottish seaside resort and becomes a lodger with the Murrays? With his father away in the Gulf, Nick Murray is more than a little disturbed by Ed Black's presence in his home – especially since he seems to have known his mother in the past.

But as Nick strikes up a friendship with the stanger and learns more about him, he also becomes aware of the terrible dilemmas that can be posed when family ties confront personal relationships.

SUMMER OF THE WAREHOUSE

Sally Bicknell

Every night before going to bed Kim Nelson looks out of his window at the warehouse which overshadows his home, and at the back of Wharf Lodge, home of an important Whitehall official.

One night he sees a man slipping quietly out of the back door of Wharf Lodge and hears Old Roberts, from down the street, accosting him drunkenly. Suddenly there is complete silence, and Kim thinks he must have been dreaming. But the next day Old Roberts is fished out of the Thames . . .

Kim's struggles to come to terms with reality plunge him into a frightening world of violence, secrecy and espionage in this lively thriller which will be enjoyed by readers of nine and over.

REBECCA'S WORLD

Terry Nation

Rebecca, mysteriously transported to a distant planet through her father's astral telescope, sets out on an exciting adventure to the Forbidden Lands in search of the last Ghost tree.

This is a rich and often funny fantasy for younger readers by Terry Nation, the creator of the Daleks.

'Undoubtedly the funniest, most imaginative children's book to have appeared in many years.'

London Evening News

If you're an eager Beaver reader, perhaps you ought to try some more of our exciting titles. They are available in book-shops or they can be ordered directly from us. Just complete the form below and enclose the right amount of money and the books will be sent to you at home.

THE SUMMER OF THE WAREHOUSE	Sally Bicknell	£1.25	☐
THE GOOSEBERRY	Joan Lingard	£1.25	☐
PONIES IN THE PARK	Christine Pullein-Thompson	95p	☐
SAVE THE HORSES!	Alexa Romanes	£1.00	☐
THE BUGBEAR	Catherine Storr	95p	☐
WHITE FANG	Jack London	£1.25	☐
GHOSTLY AND GHASTLY	Barbara Ireson, Ed	£1.25	☐
MY FAVOURITE ESCAPE STORIES	P. R. Reid, Ed	95p	☐
THE BEAVER BOOK OF REVOLTING RHYMES	Jennifer and Graeme Curry, Ed	£1.00	☐
RHYME TIME and RHYME TIME 2	Barbara Ireson, Ed	£1.50	☐

And if you would like to hear more about Beaver Books, and find out all the latest news, don't forget the BEAVER BULLETIN. If you just send a stamped self-addressed envelope to Beaver Books, 17-21 Conway Street, LONDON W1P 6JD, we will send you one.

If you would like to order books, please send this form, and the money due to:

HAMLYN PAPERBACK CASH SALES, PO BOX 11, FALMOUTH, CORNWALL, TR10 9EN.

Send a cheque or postal order, and don't forget to include postage at the following rates: UK: 45p for the first book, 20p for second, 14p thereafter to a maximum of £1.63; BFPO and Eire: 45p for first book, 20p for second, 14p per copy for next 7 books, 8p per book thereafter; Overseas: 75p for first book, 21p thereafter.

NAME...

ADDRESS...

....

PLEASE PRINT CLEARLY